# crackɘd

## K. M. WALTON

Simon Pulse

New York  London  Toronto  Sydney  New Delhi

This book is a work of fiction. Any references to historical events,
real people, or real locales are used fictitiously. Other names, characters, places,
and incidents are the product of the author's imagination, and any resemblance
to actual events or locales or persons, living or dead, is entirely coincidental.

SIMON PULSE
An imprint of Simon & Schuster Children's Publishing Division
1230 Avenue of the Americas, New York, NY 10020
First Simon Pulse hardcover edition January 2012
Copyright © 2012 by K. M. Walton
For information about special discounts for bulk purchases,
please contact Simon & Schuster Special Sales at 1-866-506-1949
or business@simonandschuster.com.
The Simon & Schuster Speakers Bureau can bring authors to your live event.
For more information or to book an event contact the Simon & Schuster Speakers Bureau
at 1-866-248-3049 or visit our website at www.simonspeakers.com.
Designed by Mike Rosamilia
The text of this book was set in Adobe Garamond Pro.
Manufactured in the United States of America
2  4  6  8  10  9  7  5  3  1
Library of Congress Cataloging-in-Publication Data
Walton, K. M. (Kathleen M.)
Cracked / by K. M. Walton. — 1st Simon Pulse hardcover ed.
p. cm.
Summary: When Bull Mastrick and Victor Konig wind up in the same
psychiatric ward at age sixteen, each recalls and relates in group therapy the
bullying relationship they have had since kindergarten, but also facts about
themselves and their families that reveal they have much in common.
ISBN 978-1-4442-2916-1
[1. Emotional problems—Fiction. 2. Family problems—Fiction.
3. Bullies—Fiction. 4. Self-esteem—Fiction. 5. Psychotherapy—Fiction.
6. High schools—Fiction. 7. Schools—Fiction.] I. Title.
PZ7.W177Cr 2012
[Fic]—dc23
2011010340
ISBN 978-1-4442-2918-5 (eBook)

*To my mom, Mary Anne Becker-Sheedy,*

*this dedication is a drop in the bucket.*

*An ocean full of drops wouldn't be enough to thank you*

*for your unwavering belief in me.*

# Victor

I HAVE WISHED THAT BULL MASTRICK WOULD DIE almost every single day. Not that I would ever have anything to do with his death. I'm not a psychopath or some wacko with collaged pictures of him hanging in my room and a gun collection. I'm the victim.

Bull Mastrick has tortured me since kindergarten. I'm sixteen now, and I understand that he's an asshole and will always be an asshole. But I wish a rare sickness would suck the life out of him or he'd crash on his stupid BMX bike and just die.

Lately, as in the past two years of high school, he's been absent a lot. Each day that he's not in school I secretly wait for the news that he's died. A sudden tragic death. As in, not-ever-coming-back-to-school-again dead. Then I'd have some peace. I could stop looking over my shoulder every five seconds and possibly even digest my lunch. Bull has a pretty solid track record of being a dick, so death is my only option.

Last year Bull pantsed me in gym. Twice. The first time was—and I can't believe I'm even allowing myself to think this, but—the first time wasn't that bad. It was in the locker room and only two other guys saw me in my underwear. And they're even more untouchable than I am. They're what everyone calls "bottom rungers."

Fortunately, the bottom rungers just dropped their eyes and turned away.

But a few weeks later Bull put a little more thought and planning into it. He waited until we were all in the gym, all forty-five of us, and when Coach Schuster ran back to his office to grab his whistle, Bull grabbed my shorts and underwear and shouted, "Yo, look! Is it a boy or a girl?"

I'm not what anyone would categorize as dramatic, but it seriously felt like he grabbed a little of my soul. I remember standing there like a half-naked statue—not breathing or blinking—as wisps of *me* leaked out of my exposed man parts. I heard a snort, which unfroze me. I slowly bent down,

K. M. Walton

pulled up my underwear and shorts, and walked back into the locker room.

And puked in the corner like a scolded animal.

He got suspended for it, which earned me two guaranteed Bull-free days in a row. You think that would've made me feel better. But each time I walked down that hallway in school or thought of the forty-five fellow ninth graders—eighteen of them girls—seeing my balls, I would gag. Then I'd run to the closest bathroom and regurgitate perfectly formed chunks of shame and disgrace.

Bull has a habit of triggering my body functions. In second grade, he made me pee my pants on the playground. He sucker punched me, and I landed face-first in a pile of tiny rocks. Bull squatted down just so he could use my head to push himself back up, squishing the rocks further into my face. He had just enough time to tell everyone I'd peed my pants before the playground monitor wandered over to see what the commotion was.

"Victor pissed his pants! Victor pissed his pants!" Bull shouted over and over again.

I laid facedown for as long as I could. I knew I'd peed my pants. I felt the warm humiliation spread through my tan shorts. And I knew that as soon as I stood up, the difference in color would be a blinking arrow, alerting the entire playground that yes, Victor Konig *had* just pissed his pants.

I got up on my elbows and felt my cheeks. It was as if my face sucked up those rocks like they were nutrients or something. Many were embedded and had to be popped out by the school nurse. I looked like I had zits—twenty-three red, oozing zits.

My father wanted to know what I had done to provoke "that boy"—like Bull was actually human. My mother only cared about what the adults at the school thought of her eight-year-old son pissing his pants. She said it made her look bad and that grown-ups would think she wasn't raising me correctly.

"Only weird boys pee their pants on the playground," she said. And then she asked me if I was weird.

She actually asked me, "Victor, are you one of those weird boys? Are you? You can't do that to Mommy. I've worked very hard to get where I am in this community, to live in this lovely neighborhood and in this beautiful home. I can't have my only child embarrassing me. Do you understand, Victor? I can't have you be one of those *weird* boys."

I remember apologizing for embarrassing her.

Bull cut in front of me in the lunch line the next day. He shoved me and said, "Out of my way, pee boy."

I remember apologizing to him, too.

K. M. Walton

# Bull

I'M KIND OF EMBARRASSED TO ADMIT THIS, BUT when I was little I thought my grandfather had an important name. I call him Pop, but he is Mr. George Mastrick. I used to think it sounded like a banker or businessman. But I'm sixteen now, and I know the only important things about my pop are his fists. They're big and they hurt. But I'd never tell him that.

I even used to think my name, William Mastrick, made me sound like I mattered. My pop renamed me Bull when I was five—said he didn't want me getting any crazy ideas that I was special. He said I wrecked everyone's life when I came along, like a bull in a china shop. The name stuck.

I know I look like my pop did when he was younger. Not from any pictures or anything. We're not the kind of family that has photo albums or memory books or any of that senti-mental crap. There isn't one photo of me till I hit kindergar-ten, and it's the school's photo anyway.

Ever since I can remember, whenever my mom has a load on, she smacks me in the side of the head and tells me how much I look like Pop.

"Dad, look, you two have the same blue eyes." It comes out like this, though: "Dah, luh, yeww teww hah the say gree eye."

My pop always tells her to shut up.

I never say a word.

We used to have the same brown hair, too. Whatever. I keep my hair buzzed, just so I won't look like him. Even though he's all gray now, we still look a lot alike, and I hate looking like him.

Pop has always hated me. At least I know where I stand. In a wacked-out way, I can appreciate that. I stay out of his way and he stays out of mine . . . unless he wants to beat the shit out of me. Then we spend some real quality time together.

I also have an uncle, Sammy, my mom's brother, who dropped out of high school when he was sixteen to become a mechanic. Turns out he couldn't hack that so he decided to become a professional druggie and alkie instead. He's pretty deep in the drug scene—spent some time in juvie for dealing weed, then big-boy jail.

When he's not locked up, he lives in a well-known drug house two blocks over from me. Which is great when you're walking home from school and your wasted uncle comes crawling out from under a neighbor's bush, covered in his own puke, asking you for money. Makes you really popular with the other kids. He hasn't been around our apartment in ages, though. I overheard his drunken dad, my grandfather—Mr. George Mastrick, Pop—on the phone with the police a few weeks ago. He's back in jail.

Now I don't want you to think that I live in a place where a drunk guy crawling out of a bush would be a shocking neighborhood event. I don't live where ladies do lunch and gossip about the vomit-covered gentleman who fell asleep in Ms. Ashley's rosebush. Hell no. I live in the dumps, a real shithole.

It's just me, Pop, and my mom all jammed together in a two-bedroom, second-floor apartment in a crappy twin house. I shouldn't say it's just me, Pop, and my mom, because that would be lying. We have tons of other things living with us. A couple hundred roaches join us every night when we turn off the lights, and we have a pack of mice that live underneath our kitchen sink. When I go to grab a trash bag from that cabinet

I am always grossed out by the mouse turds. There are piles and piles under there.

You'd think my mother would sweep them up. Try to keep her kid safe from the germs. One time, when I was little, she tried to serve me a piece of bread with a mouse turd on it, stuck in the butter. I started crying because I knew what it was. She smacked me in the back of my head and screamed that I better freakin' eat it or she'd shove it down my throat.

Yeah, she shoved the whole piece into my seven-year-old mouth and held my mouth shut until I chewed and swallowed it.

She's a real great mom.

She loves reminding me that I was never supposed to have been born. That I stole her dreams. She never really had dreams. I inherited that from her, I guess.

Her stupid big dream was to be a yoga instructor. I don't think that's even a real job. She said I wrecked her "core strength" and she would never get any respect as a real yoga professional with a pouch for a stomach. The doctors had to cut me out of her, so she's got a scar, too—which means no bikinis for her either. Yeah, also my fault.

I don't even know why she continues to throw that in my face. I swear, she acts like *I* put the guy's privates inside her that night under the Ocean City boardwalk. She hasn't

K. M. Walton

been back to the beach since that summer, so who cares if she can't wear a bikini anymore? She got fat, too. Not like enormous fat, but enough to give her an extra chin and a tire roll around her middle. After I came along, she stopped exercising because she had to work to support me and my diaper/formula addiction.

She pretty much blames me for just about every bad thing in her pathetic life. Like never graduating high school. Instead she got a job behind the desk at the local Salvation Army—Salvy to those who work there.

Salvy's a huge warehouse where rich people drop off their used shit to make themselves feel like they're contributing to society. You know, giving back. You can get crap furniture, crap kitchen stuff, crap house stuff, crap clothing, and crap shoes. That part always makes me sick. You have to be in the complete shithouse to want to buy someone else's used shoes. I don't care how rich the people are who drop off their used shoes, they still sweat and have funk between their toes. But my mom doesn't care. Every single pair of shoes she owns was worn by someone else's feet.

When I was little, she said I wore other kid's shoes all the time. She said I didn't care. I always tell her it's because I was too freakin' little to know the difference. She says I think I'm better than her. Then she wants to know, Who do I think I am? Do I think I'm some kind of rich kid? Some kind of snot? Do I really think I'm better than her?

I always tell her no, I'll buy my own freaking shoes because I'm just not stupid enough to put on someone else's rotten shoes.

Then she hits me.

I usually just let her hit me. I don't duck or cover or anything. I just let her hit me. It pisses her off so bad. When I was little, I used to cry and whimper like a baby. But I figured out fast that my pop likes to finish what my mom starts. To shut me up. And he hits a lot harder.

I know I could knock her out with one punch. I've imagined how it would go a million times. I'd smile. I'd lift my right arm, fist tight, then I'd connect with her stupid face. Down she'd go like a falling tree, cut at the base. But I never do it. The only thing mom taught me was to never hit girls. She said men who hit girls are weak, and I'm not weak. I'm the exact opposite. I can kick any kid's ass, always could.

I got in my first fight at day care. I was four years old, and the other kid wouldn't get off the swing. I didn't even ask him, I just pushed him off, and then punched him in the gut to make sure he didn't get back up. It worked. The swing was all mine.

I fought my way through elementary school and middle

school. My nose has been broken, my pinky on my right hand has been snapped the wrong way, and my lip's been ripped open a bunch of times. We've never had health insurance, not even welfare. My pop says he doesn't want any government handouts. And no daughter of his is going to stand in line like an animal for free anything.

So my nose is crooked and my pinky hurts when it rains, which is a real pain in my ass. But people leave me alone. I'm sort of over beating kids up.

Sort of.

# Victor

MY PARENTS DON'T BELIEVE IN PHYSICAL VIOLENCE.
I've never been spanked or shaken or smacked. They think it's
for poor people. Or, as my dad calls them, animals.

They don't believe in affection, either. I've always believed
they would make excellent robots. When I was little I used
to pretend they *were* robots. I imagined them landing their
spaceship somewhere in the field just outside of town and
then stumbling upon me. In my daydream, baby-me was
always wrapped in blankets, tucked in a basket on the side
of the road.

My mother would say, in perfect automaton, "Look what

I found. I think it is some sort of Earth baby. What should we do?"

My dad would reply, in his even better staccato robot voice, "We should take it. We will raise it as our own. It will teach us how to be human."

My alien fantasy doesn't work, though, because I have my mother's brown eyes and the rest of me definitely looks like my dad. Tall and skinny, brown hair. My dad is a plain, preppy-looking guy, and I'm a plain, preppy-looking guy thanks to him.

I have never seen my parents hug or kiss, or even shake hands, for that matter. They just exist on our 2.5 acres in our big, five-bedroom, three-and-a-half-bath colonial, with its granite countertops and wall-papered walls. We live separate lives in this house, in separate rooms, doing separate things. Except they are always together, and I'm always alone. My parents like to sit in the family room and read—my father in the antique, overstuffed chair and my mother on the eleven-thousand-dollar sofa.

How do I know the sofa cost eleven thousand dollars? When I was twelve years old I tried being a reader. I thought it might make my parents realize I existed. You know, give us something to talk about together. I had gotten a book out from the school library the day before. The house was quiet and my parents were out shopping—the perfect opportunity to dive into the book and be mentally armed, ready to regale them with my brilliance at lunch.

I grabbed my book and a can of Coke from the fridge. I knew I was breaking my mother's cardinal rule: Absolutely No Eating or Drinking in Any Other Rooms of This House, Except the Kitchen or Dining Room. She says that people are meant to eat at tables like civilized human beings, and that people who eat and drink while hunched over their coffee table are no better than rats in the sewers.

I sat down on the sofa, cracked opened my book and then my soda. After two sips I must have gotten lost in the story, because the can slipped from my hand. Coke dribbled out in a fizzy puddle. Of course the sofa was cream-colored, like the flesh of a pear, and Coke is brown . . . dark brown.

My mother arrived home just as I jumped up and tried to blot the puddle with my shirt hem, which just made the stain spread. My mom screamed.

Like I said, my parents don't use physical violence; they don't need to. They've mastered verbal violence.

With enough volume to make me drop the can again, splashing more Coke on the sofa, she yelled, "What are you doing, Victor? Why are you in here? With soda? Look what you've done, you . . . you monster! You monster. That sofa cost your father and I eleven thousand dollars. Eleven thousand dollars! Do you even know how much money that is? Get out! Get out! Get out!"

My mother was on the phone with upholstery cleaners in, like, two seconds, explaining how her monster of a son got soda all over her sofa, and did they know that it was an eleven-thousand-dollar sofa, and how fast could they get here, and how sweet they were for coming right away, and on and on and on. They got the stains out.

I don't read anymore, unless I have to for school. I don't go in the living room anymore either. I stay in my room and my parents stay in their living room. It all works out for us.

They don't bug me except to ensure my grades are, as my dad calls them, "top notch." He likes to say that a boy with my upbringing, my impeccable genes, my social status, should have top-notch grades. No excuses. Especially excuses that show weakness. Like sickness or a headache, or when your face gets shoved into a pile of tiny stones and you pee your pants in front of the whole second-grade playground. Or when that same asshole pushes your face into the bathroom tile and holds it there, calling you Victoria in front of four other guys, while you're trying to take a pee at the urinal right before your math final.

Nope, they are just excuses for not getting top-notch grades, excuses that show weakness.

I am weak.

# Bull

MY POP IS ON A TEAR WHEN I GET HOME FROM SCHOOL today. He has a pretty good load on, and his white T-shirt already has dribbles of gold down the front.

Did you know when beer dries on white T-shirts, it dries light gold?

I know.

By the looks of the trash can, he's had almost a full case of Mountain Crest's finest. But I can always tell by his hands. If they're open, he's not drunk. If they're shut tight into fists, he's drunk.

Both of his hands are clenched.

"You kill your granmaaah. My Bonnee. She nev hah heart prob before you . . . you . . . you were born!" he shouts in his slurred drunk-talk.

I duck to avoid getting pegged with a crushed beer can.

"Come on, Pop. Let's get you to bed," I say. If I can get him to pass out before he starts swinging, I'm usually pretty good.

"Don't tell me what I . . . what I should do."

My Uncle Sammy must be out of prison again. I see that he was here today. The kitchen table is covered in various weed paraphernalia. My pop doesn't do drugs. My mom doesn't either. I frequently question why I don't.

"What did Uncle Sammy want, Pop?" I ask, hoping to get him to unclench his fists and climb into bed.

No luck.

Just saying Uncle Sammy's name is enough to make him snap. Pop flies out of his chair and is on me before I have time to cover my face.

"Don't you ask me 'bout Sam! Don't you ask me nothin', you moron. You ruined my life," he growls.

Each word is delivered with a matching punch. My pop is really good at making words hurt, bruise, and bleed. He eventually collapses in a heap. I leave him there, passed out, and stumble to the bathroom to check out the damage. Not too bad. Most of his punches landed on my body, but he did manage to split my left cheek. Which means questions from adults at school.

I yell at myself for not covering my head. I punch the bathroom sink with self-hatred.

I look at my reflection and give myself the business. "You're so stupid! You're a freakin' idiot! You're a fucking asshole idiot!"

I am supposed to be at work in twenty minutes. I find a Band-Aid in the medicine cabinet and get my story straight.

BMX crash. Tried to jump a curb. Kid got in my way. Did a face-plant.

Blood has dripped onto my T-shirt, so I rip through the closet looking for a clean one. It's piled about waist-high with bags of shit, mostly from Salvy, but some of those bags have my clothes in them. My mom usually takes a trash bag full of clothes to the laundromat whenever she has enough change to get a load through the washer and the dryer. That's about once every two or three weeks, sometimes longer—depends if there's any leftover money after beer and cigarettes.

The woman has her priorities.

Still no clean laundry bag, and half the junk is now piled outside of the closet. I pull out a brown paper grocery bag that's rolled shut.

Did you ever see a brown paper bag that's been rolled and

K . M . Walton

rerolled so many times, it gets all soft and actually stays rolled shut? This bag stays rolled shut. Until I open it.

Inside there is a black gun. I don't know anything about guns, other than the stuff I've seen on TV and in the movies. I don't know what kind of gun it is. I just know it's a gun, and it's real. I can tell by how heavy it feels in my hand.

Pop grunts on the floor behind me.

I jump, drop the gun back into the paper bag, and close it.

He's still passed out. I stuff the bags of clothes back into the closet. I have a problem: Where should I put the brown bag? I have no place of my own—no bedroom, no closet, no dresser. I have a sofa that smells like a urinal, and that's it. I run my hand over my head and scope out my mom's room. She's got a dresser and a bed. That's it for her room.

I turn around and look into Pop's room. Twin bed, nightstand, and bags of my dead grandmother's clothes. And that's it for his room. The bag of clean laundry is in there, though. It's sitting on his bed. He must've forgotten to put it back in the closet.

And he calls *me* a moron.

But I'm a moron with a gun now.

# Victor

MY DOG DOESN'T THINK I'M WEAK.

She's a dark brown teacup poodle that my mother got the year before I was never supposed to be born. My mom used to call me My Little Accident. I guess she thought it was a nice thing to say. Maybe not—maybe she knew how despicable it was to call her son that. Who knows? She's a mystery to me most times.

Now she calls me My Accident. She gets such pleasure from telling me that I was never planned. She never wanted kids. Ever. She had too much to do with her life, she said. Like travel and shop and impress people. I didn't even come along till she was forty-one. The way I figure it, she stopped whatever birth control she was on (which is something I really don't like thinking about, but whatever) and she thought she *couldn't* get pregnant. But apparently, from the great beyond, I had other plans. Why my soul insisted on being born to two loveless robots is something I've thought about a lot in my sixteen years. Yet here I am. Her Little Accident. Sweet, sweet motherly love.

My mother got the dog for her fortieth birthday, for herself. She said she deserved something fluffy to love. I guess since I never had fur, she figured she didn't have to love me when I came along. She named the dog Jasmine, as in Jasmine tea. You know, because she's a teacup poodle? I call her Jazzer to infuriate my mom. It works like a charm.

Jazzer really does fit in the palm of my hand; she's that small. She loves me more than both of my parents combined, because she's smart enough to understand what real love is. I really love her, and she knows it. I talk to her a lot, and she listens.

Some days she's the only out-loud interaction I have. My parents are both gone when I get up, off to their important jobs where they do their important things. Jazzer always wakes me up and pays attention when I talk—not that I talk much, but when I have something to say, I say it to her, and she listens to me.

When I get home from school, she's waiting for me in the window, sitting on the sill like a statue. We have this routine where I poke her and she comes alive and jumps into my hand. Then I put her on my shoulder and she stays there while I do my homework.

One time, when I was in fourth grade, I swore Jazzer whispered, "Love you" in my ear as I finished up my hero essay. I remember foolishly telling my mother, and she laughed *at* me, not with me . . . *at* me. She called me ridiculous and then asked if I was on drugs. I was ten years old. She's perfected the art of making me feel like an idiot.

She's not my hero. Neither is my dad.

One of my heroes is definitely this guy named Johann Carl Friedrich Gauss. I did a project on him in second grade. He's called the Prince of Mathematics. For real. He was from Germany, and I'm German. Well, my dad's German and my mom is half German. She tells everyone she's pure German, though, because she's embarrassed by her mother's Irish heritage. She says the Irish left their own country because of weakness while the Germans were busy conquering the whole blessed world. She says that to her own mother. To her face.

My mother loves to tell people that our last name, Konig, means "king" in German. Like people care about our last name. She'd have made the perfect Nazi wife.

Johann Carl Friedrich Gauss and I both corrected our father's math calculations at the age of three. I used to love sneaking into my dad's office upstairs. He never knew I would go in there. I was forbidden to "go near his work." He made that very clear with his tone and word choice. But I loved climbing up to look at his architecture plans. They were always so neat, so perfect, so symmetrical, all spread out on his drafting board.

I remember finding that miscalculation in my father's math. It jumped out at me like a pop-up clown from a box, waving its hands, shouting, "I'm wrong! I'm wrong!" I went over it and over it in my head and kept getting the same answer—a different answer from my father's.

I was so lost in the math that I didn't hear the shower turn off or the bathroom door open or my father's feet pad down our handmade oriental hall rug. What I did hear was the sharpness and volume of his voice when he said, "Victor! Get down!"

He shouted with such ferocity that I lost my footing and fell off of his work stool and onto the hardwood floor. Hard.

My fall didn't faze him. No *Are you all right, son?* or *Did you hurt yourself, son?* He continued right on with his tirade. "This is my work. My work, Victor! This is not a playroom! Look around; do you see any toys in here?"

I shook my three-year-old head and rubbed my own knees.

"Get up, you little . . . little . . . pest." He spit out that part with pure disgust. "Get out of here. This is *my* office, Victor!"

I got up and walked to my room without saying a word. I knew when to keep my mouth shut. It's amazing how smart young kids are and how fast they learn.

I never did tell my dad about his error, but I heard him complaining to my mother the next night at dinner. I actually remember my three-year-old chest silently puffing with pride that night at dinner. I was right, my math was right, and he was wrong. My dad had made a mistake, and I knew it before he did.

That's when I knew I was good at math. Like, mind-blowingly good. And after my project, I knew I was good like Johann Carl Friedrich Gauss, the Prince of Mathematics. I used to call myself that in the quiet of my own head. It felt really comforting to imagine that I was the prince of something. It made me feel like I mattered, that I was important, that I was special.

I was a prince.

At first I thought being good at math would make my parents love me. At least they could brag about me, I thought. You would think people with such a superior attitude would've put their son in a fancy private school so they could brag about that, too. No luck there. My mother has this deep-seated belief that *their* hard-earned money should be spent on things involving them, and that public school is just fine for me. Besides, private or public school, all my math talent did was add more pressure. My parents love raising the bar for me, making my current achievements only *good*, never good enough.

Like today, after school, both of my parents are home early in anticipation of my SAT scores. Actually they were waiting for me when I walked in. The full 800 points I receive on the math section of the SAT isn't good enough. Out of the almost 1.5 million kids who took the test with me, only 0.7 percent scored a perfect 800 on the math. I am one of the 0.7 percent. The prince. But because I earned a 650 on the Critical Reading and 610 on the Writing, I am told that I have embarrassed my parents.

My mother makes an early dinner. It was supposed to be a celebratory dinner.

"Victor, I wish you would've prepared us for your low scores on the Critical Reading and Writing portions of your test," my mother says. She sits with her hands on her lap, back straight. She's hardly touched her food. Oh, she is so concerned.

I tell her, "I got a perfect score on the math."

She doesn't care. "Victor, how could you let those other scores happen . . . to us? It's embarrassing."

I have no answer for her. I stare at my broiled filet and wild mushroom risotto.

My father tries a stab at answering for me. "I think someone at this table has not put forth the necessary effort he needs to in reading and writing. I think someone at this table is lazy."

*Thanks, Dad.*

"I don't think he should come to Europe with us, Tomas. I really don't feel he deserves to go. Victor needs to stay here and get his priorities straight. I think he needs to be punished," my mom says.

"I agree, Aubrey. Well, then, that settles it."

"Good. I'm too upset to finish dinner. I think I'll take a drive, run an errand. I'm sick to my stomach over this."

She's hilarious. *She's* sick to her stomach. Pathetic.

My mother's the type of woman who just can't deal with anyone's feelings. Oh, she knows when and how to turn it on for the people she thinks matter (otherwise known as those with money), and she can yuck it up, squeeze forearms, and dab her eyes with the best of them. But it's all fake. Because she barely knows what to do with her own feelings. It's like she's a seed that got stuck while opening—like the rain stopped falling and the sun stopped shining and she's only open a crack.

My dad gets up from his end of the formal dining room table and walks down to be at my mother's side. He leans in, kisses her cheek, and says, "Darling, it'll be just you and me in Europe. Just like—" He stops himself.

I know what he was going to say.

The words sucker punch me one at a time.

Just.

Like.

Before.

Victor.

Was.

Born.

Victor Konig is down. It's a knockout.

# Bull

MY FREAKING HANDS SHAKE FOR, LIKE, FORTY-FIVE minutes. They're shaking like I'm doing it on purpose. I am an asshole.

But I made it to work on time—fresh Band-Aid, fresh T-shirt, fresh story. I'm unloading the last box from a lady's Range Rover SUV when the driver's side window slides down and her arm shoots out. She's snapping.

I stand there, staring at this perfect hand with five perfect nails, all polished up, and a big honking diamond ring on her finger. She keeps snapping. It takes me a moment to break the spell of her glittering hand. I look at her face, which is perfect too. Straight blond hair, big blue eyes—if she wasn't old, she'd be pretty hot. I'm close enough to the car to hear her mumbling to herself.

"I can't believe Tomas suggested I come here. There's obviously something wrong with this boy."

Then she snaps *and* waves her hand at the same time, and shouts to me, "Excuse me! Do you hear me? I'd like my tax receipt now. My husband said I would get a tax receipt."

I can't believe I thought she could've been hot. What a cow.

I shake my head while looking right into her eyes and say, "You have to get out of the car and get one yourself." I turn and walk away.

The woman obviously doesn't get it. Her voice is louder this time. "Excuse me? Isn't it your job to take care of the generous people who donate their goods?"

That is it. I swing the box onto my hip, pivot, and walk directly toward her open window. The look on her perfect old face is fear. By the time I take the five or so steps that put me right next to her car, her window has slid back up.

I decide I'm not taking her shit too. I've already taken adult-diaper-fulls of shit from my family today. I shout through the glass, "Lady, this job pays for my mom and Pop's beer, bought me these shoes, and my bike. That's all this job is. So, no, *my* job—*this* job—is not to take care of rich shits like you. Either get out of your carriage here and get the freakin' tax receipt yourself, or tell Tomas to come back and get it for you. Then you can shove that tax paper up your—"

She puts the SUV in reverse and peels out of the parking lot. I'm sure she's smart enough to fill in the word she didn't stick around to hear. She looked pretty smart to me.

I carelessly toss the lady's box into the holding room. Golf shoes tumble out as it lands in the corner. "Ha!" I shout to no one. Just what the poor slobs who shop at Salvy need. Golf shoes. Because they're playing so much freaking golf.

I walk back outside to find that my mother has come out for her break. Lucky me. She sits on a broken beach chair and lights up. At first she doesn't notice me. I've been out here unloading since I got to work. She scrunches her eyes. I guess she's noticing my busted cheek. She jumps up and gets in my face. "What did you say to him? Don't you know you keep your mouth shut?"

I know she's talking about my grandfather. "Nice to see you, too, Mom. Don't worry, I think he saved a case for you. He only killed one today."

She steps on her cigarette and grabs me by the throat. I am probably five inches taller than my mother, but she always has the power.

"You shut your wise ass up. You hear me, Bull? That's *my* daddy. You shut your stupid, wise ass up."

Even though my hands are in my pockets, I can feel them shaking again. Mom releases her death grip on my throat but keeps talking. "When are you going to learn? Are you some kind of retard?" She pulls out another cigarette, lights it, and takes a deep drag. "One of these days you'll learn to keep your mouth shut."

I stay silent and wish my eyes could drill holes into her skull. I wish the cigarette smoke would pour out of the holes and. . . .

"Are you listening to me? What are you, deaf? You stupid? Don't you have something to say?" she barks.

Gotta love my mom. She yells at me because she wants me to keep my wiseass mouth shut. Then she yells at me because I have nothing to say. She's a confused woman.

I shrug my shoulders and squeeze my hands into fists, pushing them deeper into my front pockets. I watch as she stands on her toes. Then she reaches up and smacks the back of my head. I instinctively pull my hand out of my pocket and rub my head.

"What did you do that for?" I ask her.

"'Cause you're a shit, that's why. A stupid shit. Don't shrug your shoulders at me either. You gonna keep your mouth shut round Pop?"

"I guess," I say.

She stubs her cigarette out, and we go our separate ways.

It isn't until the bike ride home that I figure something out: My mother was trying to protect me. She kept saying she wanted me to keep my mouth shut around Pop. Of all people, my mom knows that keeping your mouth shut around Pop means your chances of getting your ass beat drops big-time. At least that's what I think. It's the only way she knows how to look out for me, other than threaten and yell and curse and insult me.

I realize something else as I pedal: My mom taught me that guys who hit girls are weak. I know my pop doesn't feel that way. He rules his roach-infested castle with his fists. And my mom has been on the other side of his fury many times. He won't punch the ladies. That's where he draws the line. Instead, he prefers to open-hand slap, shove, and verbally beat down the loves of his life, the apples of his eye.

It's funny that my pop blames me for my grandmother's death. No, seriously, it's funny. I was half-asleep on my bed/sofa one night when my mom and him were wasted and got into a shouting match about it.

"It wasn't Bull's fault thah mom died. You shoon't tell him'nat," my mother had gargled, a beer can in one hand, a cigarette in the other.

It had taken my pop like thirty seconds to respond to that mouthful. "You gettin' knocked up like a whore unner tha boardwalk's what broke her heart."

I had squeezed my eyes shut. I remember I was nine and had known it was about to get ugly. I'd heard the crumpling of aluminum and then felt a crushed can pelt me in the calf.

"That kid cryin' every single goddamn second of its life is what killed my Bonnee. First you broke her heart, and then *he* killed her."

I'd heard a chair slide across the kitchen floor, and then my mom screaming, "You killed Mommy! You killed her. Not me, not Bull. You beat her up the day before. I saw you do it! She hit her head when you shoved her. I . . . I . . . saw."

I'd opened my eyes to a squint—I didn't want either of them knowing I was awake. I'd watched my drunk mom pound on Pop's arms and back, and then slide down onto the floor while he just sat there. He hadn't hit her back. He'd drained his beer, crushed the can against the table, and threw it directly at me, again. That time it hit my foot, but I'd stayed perfectly still.

I distinctly remember having to swallow the smile that had threatened to form on my fake-sleeping face. Up until that moment, I had been convinced that I really had killed my own grandmother. That she really had died from nonstop infant crying. It had been pounded into my skull for nine years. Kids believe what their parents tell them. Kids believe what their grandfathers tell them even more. And my grandfather had a way with words.

I actually had to turn over on the sofa to face the wall so I could let the smile out. *I didn't kill my grandmother. It wasn't my fault. My pop killed her, not me.* I'd repeated it that night until I fell asleep.

It had ended up being a pretty decent night for me.

# Victor

I HAD BEEN LOOKING FORWARD TO EUROPE. NOT TO spending quality bonding time with Mom and Dad, but to getting away from them. They were happiest when I wasn't around. My presence always seemed to snuff out their candles. So I planned to abandon them as much as possible and wander Europe by myself. I had crafted my setups weeks ago.

*Mom, Dad, why don't you two go to breakfast (or lunch, or dinner) together and relax?*

*Mom, Dad, I'm going to stay back today and work on these calculus workbooks I packed. You two go on and spend time together.*

Last night's decision to disinvite me was absolute. My mother left me a note on the counter this morning telling me my airline ticket had already been cancelled. She ended her note with, *P.S. I'm so disappointed in you.*

Feel the love.

During my walk to school, I realize my parents will leave for their trip two days into summer vacation, which is in a week. I am certain they will dream up insane amounts of schoolwork as part of my punishment while they slide down the canals of Venice and sip expensive French wine. And then I realize I'll be rid of them for fourteen days—in a row. Fourteen days is a long, long time.

A horrible thought stabs my happy balloon. What if they fly my grandmother up to watch me? Oh, God.

"Move, Victoria!" Bull screams into my ear as he rides by me on his bike in the parking lot. He pedals like he's being chased by the devil, jumps the curb, throws his right arm backward, and gives me the finger. And then he's gone round the corner, out of sight. I wish for him to get hit by a car. For a parent not paying attention as they leave the parking lot to smash right into him. With each step, I long to hear the sound of screeching tires and screams of pain.

No crash. His stupid bike's chained up.

He finds me at lunch, too.

"Asshole, you're in my seat," he says.

This, of course, is an impossibility. I don't ever sit in the same seat twice. I move. I scout out places where I can be alone. I just want to be left alone. Today I chose a seat in the far left corner, facing the window, facing away from the tables of laughter and friendship.

He repeats, "Asshole, you're in my seat."

I decide to ignore him. I can see other available seats. And I reason that silence works on my parents, and they're Albert Einsteins compared to his amoeba brain. I want it to appear as if I don't care. That Bull calling me an asshole means nothing to me. So I take a sip of my chocolate milk and ignore him.

Bad idea.

I wish at that moment I had chosen to face the cafeteria, so my back wasn't to Bull. His beastlike fist lands midway down my back. The punch must've been subtle, fast enough to go unnoticed in this cafeteria of happiness.

His punch makes my body do two embarrassing things. First, I spit my mouthful of chocolate milk all over the table, ending with a magnificent crescendo of dribble and effectively chocolate-milking the front of my white golf shirt. Second, I choke. The chocolate milk that had already passed the back of my throat, in a defiant swallow, decides to suffocate me.

I can't breathe. At all. Instinctively, my hands go to my chest and I try to punch air back into me.

Bull can only see the back of my head. He can't see my bulging eyes filling with genuine panic. I still can't breathe. He thinks I'm ignoring him.

"You're dead, Victoria."

I think he may be right.

In one fast motion, he slams my head into my plate of French fries and I'm out cold.

Guess what I see?

Me, with a crown and a red cape lined with white fur, holding a jeweled scepter in my left hand and shaking the hand of Johann Carl Friedrich Gauss with my right. I'm in Germany. I've time-traveled back to the eighteen hundreds to meet Johann, which has always been my wish. This is so real. He's telling me I'm the new Prince of Mathematics. There's a crowd, a huge crowd, and they're all cheering my name. "Vic-tor! Vic-tor! Vic-tor! Vic . . ."

Except someone is shaking me.

"Victor! Are you okay?"

It's not Bull. He's long gone. Actually, most of the cafeteria is empty. There are just a few stragglers left. Patty Cullen is shaking and talking to me.

"I think you passed out, Victor. Do you want me to walk you to the nurse?"

K. M. Walton

I say no.

She pulls a flattened French fry from my forehead.

I say thank you.

Out of the entire school I *am* thankful it was Patty Cullen who revived me and removed the fry.

She smiles gently and tells me it's no big deal.

I wish I could smile back. This is the first time she's said a word to me since we had to do that science project together in eighth grade.

She asks me one more time if I'm really okay. I nod. She nods back and then walks away.

I'm alone and alive and covered in chocolate milk.

But I still feel like I'm dead.


Patty Cullen must've kept quiet about me passing out into my French fries, because no one asks me about lunch. Who knows if she even saw what Bull did to me? As I walk through the hall to go grab a sweatshirt from my locker, not one teacher or student asks me what is on my shirt, or what happened, or a single question about anything. It's amazing how invisible I am to everyone at school, except Bull.

My first-grade strategy of keeping to myself and staying quiet has really worked. One kid, Andrew Quinn, tried to strike up a friendship with me in second grade. At first I'd entertained the thought. It had felt good to have a kid look at me, you know, really see me. We'd played together for an entire week. Then he had asked me to come over to his house and play.

My parents had effectively ended the friendship when they found out Andrew lived on the other side of town in an apartment. And he only had a dad. No mom. My mother forbade me from "socializing" with him. She'd told me she had hired the cafeteria workers to report back to her if they saw me playing with him.

I'd believed her.

I remain invisible to kids.

Of course, I come home to an empty house. Empty of people. Jazzer greets me like I am her hero. Her prince. Jazzer always sees me.

"Hey, girl. Come on," I say and then scoop her into my hand.

We climb the stairs as one. As soon as I open the laundry-room door, I strip off my humiliation-stained shirt, spray the heck out of it with stain stuff, and get a load of laundry going. I let Jazzer sit on my bare neck; she feels so warm and soft.

She's the only one whom I'd consider a friend. Which is pathetic for obvious reasons, like she's a dog, but also because she's eighteen years old. Teacup poodles usually only live for around eleven or twelve years. My one and only friend is on borrowed time. I did some research online and found a blog by this couple whose teacup poodles made it all the way to nineteen and twenty years old. I visit their blog at least once a week just to read that one post.

"Jazzer, you're a good girl, Jazz," I say. She licks my earlobe, like usual, and nuzzles her tiny head right under my ear. It's her thing.

I walk out of the laundry room and across the hall into my bedroom. My mother had one of the five bedrooms transformed into a laundry room before they even moved in. She said she refused to traverse two sets of stairs like a common maid. If I know my father, he treated the project like God himself had asked for the laundry room. My mother has that effect on him.

She likes to tell people the tale that he had it up and running— with brand-new machines, custom cabinets, imported Italian tile floor, and three thousand dollars' worth of designer wallpaper— as her welcome home gift.

Jazzer jumps off my neck and sits on my bed. I throw on a navy golf shirt and a clean pair of shorts. "Bull said I was in his seat, and then he punched me in the back today. The prick."

She tilts her head to the right. That's how I know she's listening. Her eyes never leave mine either.

"I think I died today, Jazzer. I know I passed out, but I think I crossed over to the other side. When my face was in my tray of French fries, I swear I had a vision. Like I was dead. I was the Prince."

Jazzer tilts her head to the left.

"Don't worry. I'll never leave you, Jazz," I say, and rub underneath her jaw. "Hey, you wanna go for a walk, girl?"

She's at my bedroom door before I get out the word "girl."

"I guess that's a yes."

# Bull

SCHOOL SUCKED, AS USUAL.

I'm in all the dumbass classes—and I don't mean the classes are dumb, I mean the kids who are in the classes are dumb. Some genius in charge of schools decided to lump all of the dumb kids together and have them travel around class to class, like a big, dumb, unhappy family. And then all the smart kids got shoved together. Just so we all don't forget who's dumb and who's smart. Like we dumbasses need reminding. What-the-fuck-ever.

Instead of going home after school, I ride my bike to the cemetery.

As I ride, I go over shit in my head. I'm making around one hundred dollars a week at my job. The Salvy's good to me. I give my mother fifty bucks, because she says I have to help pay for living. Like she provides a happy living, a happy home life, with food, clothing, and love. Living to her means moldy bread, clothing swiped from the donation bags before it gets tagged and hung up, sleeping on a sofa that smells like pee, and dollar-store soap—never shampoo. No, she says soap does the same job. That's how she was raised, and if using soap for shampoo is good enough for her, well then dammit, it is good enough for me.

Whether she sucks or not, I still give my mom fifty dollars, which I know goes directly into the beer distributor's hands almost immediately after it leaves mine. My mom and my pop love their beer. They drink the cheap stuff. The kind that gets them the most amount of beer for fifty dollars. They buy this crap beer called Mountain Crest, and it's $11.19 a case before tax and $11.72 after tax. Even though I suck at math, I know that fifty bucks gets them four cases of it and it's gone in less than five days. Every single week.

I take the other fifty bucks and put it through this system I designed. First, I take eight bucks and buy a new paperback book. Yeah, I know I could buy used books at Salvy for like a quarter, but I think it's worth it, because I

K. M. Walton

want to be the first person to crack the spine open. It's my favorite part.

No one knows that I read. Not my mother, not Pop, and no one at school. That's because I never do it in public. But if someone tortured it out of me, I guess I'd admit that I read because I like it. I read to clear my head, and I only read at the cemetery. And I hide my favorite books at home, underneath the sofa. I take enough shit from those two. But I do this good deed and dump my nonfaves in the book bin at work after I finish reading. I know it's goofy, but I sort of get a rush when I see someone buy one of my donated books; I like the idea of something *I* read being passed along to another reader. In a weird way I feel connected. And I suck at connecting with people.

Next, I take ten bucks and put it in my "bank." It's a gray metal box I picked up at Salvy a few years ago. I even found a lock and key, like, a year later. I keep it underneath the tallest pine tree along the back wall of the cemetery. After the third time digging up the box I realized what a moronic idea it was to bury it. So now it's just hidden really good.

No one ever goes into this cemetery. At least not in the four years I've been hiding out there. That's when I started skipping school a lot and wandering around the streets. That's also when I discovered that the police officers know who should be in school and who shouldn't. They're smart. So I had to find a place to hide. A place with no people. No live people, anyway.

I've checked out the headstones, and they're old—some of 'em you can't even read anymore. Most of the stones are from the seventeen and eighteen hundreds. The only person I've ever seen is the old guy who cuts the grass in between the headstones. He comes every single Friday, rain or shine, summer or winter, at exactly 9:15 in the morning. He scared the crap out of me the first time I saw him. I don't think he saw me, though. If he did, he never let on. I'd been sitting against one of the bigger headstones, reading the third Harry Potter book, when he walked right by me, two rows over.

Immediately I'd ducked down and stayed down. He had passed by me three more times—twice on the mower and once as he left the cemetery.

It didn't take me long to figure out his schedule, so I make sure I'm either not there when he is or I'm on the move so he doesn't see me. It works for me, and it means I'm not in school with the rest of the dumbasses.

I hide my bike behind the huge holly bush and climb through the break in the fence. It's 7:30 p.m. on a Friday, so I know the old guy's already been here. I'll be alone. I just want to breathe. In and out. A few times. And a few more times. I hold my hands out in front of me to measure how steady I am, how clear my head is.

I slide down the tree trunk and watch the day turn gray and dark, like me. I look toward my bike and smile.

It took me eleven weeks of saving my dough to buy my Haro Original Freestyler on Craigslist. I actually found some forty-year-old dude who bought it without his wife knowing, and she was pissed. He bought it because it reminded him of the bike he had in the 1970s. He told me his wife said he was going through a midlife crisis and she thought it wasn't fair for him to spend their hard-earned money on something so useless. I didn't care about him, his wife, or his stupid crisis. I just wanted his Original Freestyler.

He paid 545 bucks for it brand-new, but just wanted his wife to stop bitching at him, so he sold it to me for 350 bucks.

Can you say, "score"?

Every other bike I've ever had came from Salvy. And I've had some semigood ones over the years. But no bike can come close to my Haro. It's nicer than my mother's crappy car.

It's got chrome, and Tuff Wheels, and it's retro-gear heaven on this crap Earth. I keep it triple-locked with crazy-tough chains back behind my apartment. I don't know what it is with us poor people, but we love to steal from one another. I don't get it. And we'll steal anything that's not locked, stapled, strapped down, alarmed, or guarded. It doesn't seem to matter who owns it, just that the other person wants it. I don't know if all crap neighborhoods have to deal with stealing, but I know *my* crap neighborhood does.

So I triple-lock my Haro.

But not here. I don't lock it here. Who's gonna steal it? The old guy on the lawn mower? Don't think so.

I watch the sun disappear completely, and I sit in the dark. I'm not afraid here. It's too peaceful and quiet. I think in the dark. And I think. And Operation Freedom takes solid shape in my head.

Like, a-piece-of-frozen-dog-shit solid.

# Victor

I ROUND THE CORNER OF OUR BLOCK. JAZZER'S taking her sweet old time with this walk. She usually has a lot more zing in her step. "Come on, girl. There's Mom; she's home from work." She sits down on the neighbor's grass. "Jazz, come on."

She lies down.

"All right," I say. "Come on, I'll carry you." I walk the rest of the way home cupping Jazzer in my hand, holding her against my chest. She falls asleep.

I lay her in her bed and walk into the kitchen to find my mother.

"Hey," I say. It's the first time I've seen her since the "dinner of disappointment."

"I was almost killed yesterday. This . . . this . . . animal of a boy nearly attacked me at the Salvation Army. He used disgusting, foul language. I barely got out with my life."

I used to get sucked into my mother's madness when I was younger. She suffers from what I've named "overdramatosis." I used to worry and cry with her, and fear for her safety. In a weird way it made me feel protective of her. Not anymore. My father still falls for it, though. He falls hard and blows his warm breath onto her burning fire of craziness, and then they both burn bright and hot for a while.

"Wow," I say. "That sucks." I wish I could tell her about *my* day. About Bull and the punch and the humiliation. But I can't. And I don't.

She stops her pacing and flies up to my face. "I will not hear that type of language in my own home. You will not use that word, do you understand?"

I look down at her and say, "Fine."

I want her to walk away first, so I can go up to my room. She says she has to lie down; recalling her near-death experience has taken a toll on her. She shouts to me from the balcony, "Why is there laundry going, Victor? Was Consuelo here today? She is only contracted for four days. She wasn't supposed to come today. We need someone who speaks English clearly. I can't keep explaining things to her."

I close my eyes and let her finish before I shout back from the kitchen, "*I'm* doing laundry, Mom. Consuelo wasn't here today. And she speaks English fine."

"Don't shout to me." I hear what I think is a foot stomp, and I roll my eyes. She continues, "Come in this foyer so I can see you when you speak to me."

I do as she says.

"Now, why are you doing laundry?" she asks in her perfectly toned robot voice.

I tell her that I spilled something on my white golf shirt at lunch. I intentionally leave out that it was chocolate milk. She thinks chocolate milk is a poor person's dessert and will rot your teeth. In sixth grade I started drinking it with my school lunch, as an act of pure rebellion.

"Well, why didn't you leave it for the maid? That is her job, Victor."

I want to get in her face and tell her that she's an evil, robotic witch. I wish I had the guts to.

I just exhale and I tell her I don't know.

# Bull

MY MOM ISN'T HOME WHEN I GET BACK FROM THE cemetery, but my pop is. Except he's unconscious. He's passed out across the kitchen table. Beating the crap out of me yesterday must've tired him out. Poor guy.

I open the refrigerator and laugh to myself. I don't know why I ever bother looking in the fridge, but I still do it, like five times a day. I don't know what I expect to find. Food? Yeah, right. Only thing that's ever in there is beer. I shut the fridge and open the cabinet next to it. On the rare occasion we have some type of food, that's where it would be.

A few years ago my mom snuck off to some community-run parenting class. Now, before you get the idea that she went so she could learn how to be a better mom, let me set you straight. She went because they gave away free food each day, just for going to the class. And for the whole week that cabinet had food in it. Boxes of crackers, cookies, cereal, and noodles; cans of soup; and jars of sauce. Real food. I clearly remember standing in front of it and crying like a girl. Neither of them saw me boo-hooing, trust me; they were passed out by that time.

Tonight's food selection is the two ends of a loaf of bread in a crumpled plastic bag. That's it. No butter. I'm so hungry I almost wish we had mouse-turd butter. I eat the first bread-end in one bite. Swallow. Then the second. Dinner is served.

If you think my mom got anything out of those parenting classes, you're fucking delusional. She went hungover every day and told me she fell asleep two of the days. She said the teacher got pissed at her and asked her to leave on the last day. My mom said she yelled at her in front of the whole class of parents and said she wasn't going nowhere without her free food. She earned it. The teacher handed her a brown grocery bag, then got a huge Latino dude to escort her out of the building.

Mom was so proud of herself.

I take another look at my pop, spread out across our kitchen table, which is barely big enough for two people to sit at, and I am filled with anger. A rage boils in my gut, and it's so violent and painful that I gag.

I hate him. I used to love him; at least I think I did. But that was before I could wipe my own ass, before I knew any better. I stare down at him and let it sink in. I really hate him. I hate everything about him. And this is new for me, this clear thinking.

I hate his white, slicked-back hair; his yellow teeth; his blue eyes that used to be really blue but have turned an ugly shade of blue-gray; his beer gut; his stained white T-shirts and tan work pants.

And his hands. I really hate his hands. Those hands are weapons.

It's at this exact moment that I know, 100 fucking percent, that my life will be so much better when he is dead.

Operation Freedom is a go.

K. M. Walton

# Victor

I'M IN BED WHEN I DECIDE I'D RATHER BE DEAD than alive. It isn't that I hate the being alive part, it's that I hate my entire life and I know that not living would be a lot easier. I'm probably not making any sense. This is all new thinking for me. And I can thank my lovely mother for putting the thought in my head in the first place.

In her overly dramatic way, she retold the Salvation Army horror story at dinner.

"Tomas, please don't ask me to ever drop anything off at that wretched place ever again. That boy wanted to . . . oh, I don't know what evil was running through his small brain. But just promise me, Tomas. It was like he wanted me dead. Like having me dead would be easier than getting my tax receipt. The animal."

I let my father breathe his "Oh, Darlings" all over her fire of crazy while the words "having me dead would be easier" held a party in my head. Those six words danced and jumped and high-fived each other. They blew noisemakers and tossed colorful confetti and then danced around some more.

Having me dead would be easier!

I let the whole idea take me over as I lie in bed, Jazzer asleep on my chest.

I rationalize these new thoughts. I certainly wouldn't be leaving a group of friends behind, a girlfriend, or anyone. So I'm not being selfish. My parents never wanted me in the first place, so they'll have me out of their hair just in time for their European trip. I tell myself I'm actually doing them a favor. Because I am. I only have one grandparent, and she hasn't seen me in years. We gave up the painful phone conversations years ago, when my mom would make me call her and thank her for her birthday gift. I never knew what to say and neither did she. My mom has been calling her "forgetful" lately, so she probably wouldn't even realize I'm gone. My thoughts are making so much sense. My thinking is crystal clear.

Jazzer wakes up and slowly positions her little body right

K. M. Walton

under my left ear. She curls up into a ball and makes this tiny little yawn/squeak sound. It's the sound she makes when she is perfectly happy. I think it's the best sound in the world. And then it hits me.

Jazzer would fall apart without me. She really does love me. Then I fall apart.

I don't know where the category-five waterworks are coming from, but they are here, and I'm officially sobbing like a baby. What makes my stomach clench is the thought that my teacup poodle, who technically isn't even my dog, is the only thing, human or otherwise, that would stop me from committing suicide.

# Bull

LAST NIGHT I FELL ASLEEP CREATING VARIOUS SCENES in my mind, all ending with Pop dead. It sounds sick, I know. But I slept like a rock.

Knowing there's no food in the kitchen cabinet, I brush my teeth and am out the door pretty fast. Once I get my third bike lock undone, I'm on my way to school. Then it hits me: It's Saturday. Idiot.

Instead of listening to Pop bitch about his headache, I decide to chill at the cemetery for a while before I have to go to work at ten. After I crawl through the rusty and bent part of the black wrought-iron fence, something catches my eye. I know every single inch of this graveyard, every headstone and bush, so a brown lunch bag sitting in the exact spot I normally sit in— well, that jumps out at me real quick. It wasn't here last night.

I squat down next to the fence and let my eyes roam the whole place. The old guy's truck isn't there. Of course it isn't. It's Saturday, not Friday. Idiot. I don't see anyone or anything.

I'm alone, so I squat-crawl the ten feet over to my spot at the base of the tree and open the bag. I rummage through. It looks like someone's lunch, all packed up nice by their mommy. No sandwich, but there's a plastic bottle of fruit drink, a bag of chips, a granola bar, and an apple.

I look around again. Whoever put the bag here did it not too long ago, because the drink's still cold and covered with beads of sweat.

I'm still alone.

I dump the contents of the bag onto my lap and lift the bag to my face, just to be sure I haven't missed any food. Stuck to the bottom of the bag is a Post-it note. I reach in and peel it off so I can read it.

That's all it says. One word. And enjoy I do. At one point I have to remind myself to breathe, which helps me slow down and actually taste the food. God, the apple is good. I think about it. I haven't had a piece of fresh fruit since third grade, when Alison Smith's mother brought in a humongous bowl of fruit salad for her birthday. That was the last time. Unbelievable.

I look around again, half expecting someone to pop up and get pissed because I ate their bag of food. But no one comes. I check my box of money and count it. $376.54.

I laugh, keeping the fifty-four cents in there. That fifty-four cents has been in there for, like, four years. I decided a long time ago that I like the sound it makes when I move the box around. So it stays.

I lie back on the freshly mown grass with a full stomach and make the biggest plan of my life. I'm going to shoot my pop, and then I'll go away. Far away.

Suddenly, the $376.54 has a new purpose.

# Victor

TODAY IS SUNDAY. CHURCH DAY. PHONY FAMILY Breakfast Day. I hate this day.

"I will not walk into church late, Victor. You know the whole church watches us walk in," my mother says through my closed bedroom door.

I so want to say, *Wouldn't your life be easier without me, Mother?* But I zip up my pleated khakis and breeze by her in the hall.

"No 'good morning' for your mother?" she says after me. I am on the second from the top step when she says, "Victor! Stop right there!"

I stop and stay facing forward. An intentional act on my part to tick her off.

"You turn around right now and face me when I'm speaking to you."

I roll my eyes before I turn around.

Her voice is steely. "Now say 'good morning' to your mother before you move one more muscle."

"Good morning, Mother," I say. I bound down the rest of the staircase quickly, so I can get far away from her.

I hear her tell my dad that she is happy I'm not going to Europe with them because I disgust her. Not my crankiness or ignoring her. Me. *I* disgust her.

One thing is definite: *She* disgusts *me*.

The car ride to church is silent. For me, anyway. My parents chirp back and forth at each other like happy little robots.

"You look lovely today, Aubrey," my father says.

"Thank you, darling. So you like my dress?"

"I do, I do."

Blah, blah, blah.

I always laugh to myself on the way to church. It's not that I think church itself is funny; I think church is stupid. I laugh inside at the fact that my parents go to church every single solitary Sunday, faithfully. Same church, same time, same pew. They probably say the same prayers in their robot heads.

My mother: *Dear God, please let me impress every human being in this church.*

My father: *Dear God, please let my wife impress every human being in this church.*

Here's the funny part: The same two people who go to church each week treat their only son like a cold sore. Actually, cold sores probably get more attention, even though that attention is directed at making them go away. They still are looked at and have creams rubbed on them and maybe even get prayers directed at them. They are seen. People notice cold sores. I bet if I end up getting a perfect 2400 when I retake my SATs, my parents would find some way to screw up my victory. Nothing I do is good enough for them. Not one thing.

But they go to church every Sunday and phony-baloney it with the whole congregation. Shaking hands and patting backs; complimenting jewelry or new hairstyles; making golf dates, lunch dates, dinner plans.

Talking to people.

Noticing people.

Seeing people.

Why don't they ever see me?

I stop laughing to myself. I'm silent both inside and out now.

# Bull

SCHOOL ENDS IN ONE WEEK. I MAKE THE DECISION
to not skip. I want to make it to junior year, and I've missed a
shitload of classes this year. So sue me.

School is where I keep my postcard of the beach. It's
taped to the back of my locker. I don't need any wiseasses
thinking I'm either missing some stupid girl I met at the
beach or whatever. I just want to keep it private. Like if King
Nerd Victoria saw it, his enlarged freak brain would cook
up some story, I know it. I don't want any cooked-up stories
going around about me. Even though I don't think I've ever
seen Victor Konig talk to a single person in this school, I'm

not taking any chances. Besides, I'd pound him to a pulp if he ever said a single word about it or me.

I know my mom and Pop would call me stupid for keeping that postcard, so I've always kept it at school. I found it when I was seven, in one of my mom's old jackets, way back in the closet. The same closet as the gun.

The day I found the postcard I was digging for a clean pair of shorts, and I found a bag of my mom's old clothes buried underneath some papers. I rummaged through the bag of clothes; it was all stuff from when she was skinny. In other words, pre-me. And I found an old jean jacket of hers. I tried it on to see if it would fit, and inside one of the inner pockets was a postcard of the beach. OCEAN CITY, NEW JERSEY . . . WHERE FAMILIES GO TO THE BEACH! There was handwriting on the other side. It said:

Leslie,
I'm not ready to
be a dad. I want
you to get rid
of it.

— Steve

A man of few words, my dad.

I also need the computers at school to do research about jail time and other stuff. I'm definitely moving forward with Operation Freedom. The other decision I make is to not look Pop in the face anymore. I don't do it too often anyway, but now I really can't look into his eyes. I'm afraid he might see through me and know what I'm planning.

Yesterday, when I woke up . . . let me rephrase that. Yesterday, when *he* woke me up by grabbing my ankle and dragging me across the room, screaming that there was no goddamn food in the goddamn apartment, I landed in a weak, crumpled ball. I tried to play dead, but he yanked me up and we were eye to eye. I swear, when I stared into his eyes with murder on my mind, he knew it. And for probably the first time in my life, I felt power over him. He didn't say anything to me. He just shoved me hard into the wall, knocking the wind out of me. And as I caught my breath I could tell he knew that I wanted to kill him.

Don't ask me how, because I don't know. I could just tell.

I walk through the halls of my school and kids move out of my way. No one wants to look me in the eyes, either. I notice this today. I guess it has always been that way, but since I've got eyes on the brain, I really notice every kid dropping their gaze.

I've always really liked that kids are piss-their-pants afraid

K. M. Walton

of me. One time, in like second grade, I made Victor eat pavement, and then he pissed his pants. I literally scared the piss right out of him. It was awesome. No one talked to me for a while because they were afraid of me. But I got back into the recess games eventually.

I figured out pretty quickly that my life wasn't made for having friends. I was never allowed to go over to anyone's house, not that there were tons of invites or anything. Those dried up in, like, kindergarten. And you don't have to be a brain surgeon to figure out that I'd never invite anyone over to my apartment. Ever. So, yeah, my life isn't made for friends. I don't need friends, not when my life is so full.

So full of shit.

Study hall is the perfect place to work out the kinks of Operation Freedom. Back at the cemetery, I played around with a crapload of other names before I decided on Operation Freedom.

Operation Payback.

Operation Pop-less.

Operation Smackdown.

They all sounded stupid and mean. So I went with Operation Freedom. It makes the whole plan sound necessary and important, and not awful. I really need it to not sound awful in my head.

The first search I do is on the amount of time a juvenile could get for murder when it's in self-defense. I click on an article that says two teenagers got thirty-three years for a double murder they committed. Thirty-three years is a long time. I do the math in my head. I'd be forty-nine when I got out of jail. Only eight years younger than my pop is now. I search again.

Next article I click on is about a sixteen-year-old white supremacist that shot a fifteen-year-old in the back of the head while he was sitting in class. That kid was tried as an adult and got fifty-three years to life. Fifty-three years is twenty years longer than thirty-three years. I'd be an almost-seventy-year-old geezer when I got out.

Fuck. Operation Freedom is squashed like a roach.

# Victor

I CHOOSE A NEW CORNER IN THE CAFETERIA TODAY, and I decide to sit with my back to the wall. I don't want that idiot sneaking up on me again. Facing out into the room full of people gives me a whole new feeling.

Dread.

I watch tables, crowded with teenagers, laughing, shoving, giggling, smiling, eating, flirting, and talking. That's a lot of *ing*. And I'm not part of any of it. And I never have been. I feel queasy. The only thing I can get down is my chocolate milk, each sip an FU to mom. I push my tray of food away from me and take it all in.

If I never came back here, never walked these halls again, never ate in this caf, there isn't one person in this entire school who'd be affected. Even my math teacher would get over it. I'm just a feather in his cap; he doesn't know me. He doesn't know anything about me. All he knows is that I'm smarter than he is when it comes to anything math-related because all we've ever talked about is math.

Now, I realize I am not the most approachable person in the world. I sit here, in this corner or that corner, on purpose—so I don't have to interact with anyone. I drop my eyes, put my earbuds in my ears, and make myself fade away. I walk straight home. I don't stop at the store, or ride my bike to the park, or invite people over, or go anywhere, with anyone, at any time. I get all that.

Wow. I think I just blamed myself for being a nobody. Yep, I did. I blamed myself. How perfect. My crap life *is* all my fault.

My pity party lasts almost the entire lunch period. The sound of laugher snaps me out of my daze. I look to my left and see Patty Cullen across the way, and *she's* laughing. She sees me see her, and we stare at each other. Maybe it's the sunlight streaming down from the window behind her, but I swear that she looks like an angel. The dust particles float and dance in the light like glitter; everything seems to be in slow motion. I wish I had the guts to walk up to her table and tell her how pretty her hair looks with that headband and how nice her smile is. "Guts" is the wrong word here. Balls. I wish I had the balls to compliment her.

No one at her table notices us noticing each other. After a few seconds Patty raises her eyebrows and smiles at me. I raise my eyebrows and probably look like I just had an accident in my pants. The bell rings and the room full of *ing*-ers head out. I get up to toss my lunch tray, and when I turn around to head to class, there she is, smiling in all of her headbanded glory.

"Hey, Victor, are you okay? You know, from Friday?"

Balls, guts—neither one is making an appearance at the moment. "Yeah, fine."

"Good. I thought about you over the weekend. I was wondering if you were really okay."

She thought about me? Over the weekend? Me? I can't believe she thought about me over the weekend. She thought about—

Patty interrupts my inner astonishment with: "Okay, well, I've gotta run to French." Her mouth curls into the most adorable grin and then she blows me a kiss. *"Au revoir."*

That is that.

I take a deep breath and try to inhale her kiss. I want to feel it in my lungs, kissing me from the inside. I want to, but I can't. Instead my lungs fill with the fried stench of the cafeteria, and I instantly feel like an asshole. Who wants to be kissed on the inside?

I have a crazy thought. A stupid, crazy thought. Maybe she'd notice if I never came back. Maybe she'd care.

I huff. "Yeah, right," I say out loud.

The bell rings, and even the custodian sweeping the floor ignores me.

"Yeah, right," I repeat.

K. M. Walton

# Bull

NOT SPENDING MORE THAN A DECADE IN JAIL. even to get rid of Pop. I can't do it. I guess that makes me turd. I guess I deserve the beatings coming my way. I down and cup my balls. Yeah, they're still there. I've got alls. It's just that my balls are only good for punching dorks n the back.

But I am not weak. I'm not.

It must be the quiet in here that's making me get all psychological and shit, but I'm wondering . . . am I a murderer? I've never thought of myself as a person capable of real murder. I stare over the top of my computer, watching kids silently walk through the library, and I almost say out loud, *So, could I really have shot Pop? As in dead. Blood-gushing, brain-splattering dead?* I could've always closed my eyes when I pulled the trigger. Yeah, I wouldn't have seen the mess, but I would have known what I did. In a complete dick kind of way, my heart would've known.

I reach up and rub my skull with both hands. I wish I could just freaking disappear right now because my head is clogged up with dirt and muck and shit.

Two girls walk by the table, whispering about what bikii will make their boobs look better, and a thought smacks r right in the forehead: School is out in four days; summei here. Maybe I'll just spend the whole summer workin₉ Salvy—bump my hours to the max—and stay the hell o Pop's way. I only have two more years at home and thei out of here. Two more years. Of beatings.

I can't do it. I can't take two more years of his shit. I do know what to do. And I have to get to work.

**INJURY NOTED**

K. M. Walton

AM

Not

a re

rea

b

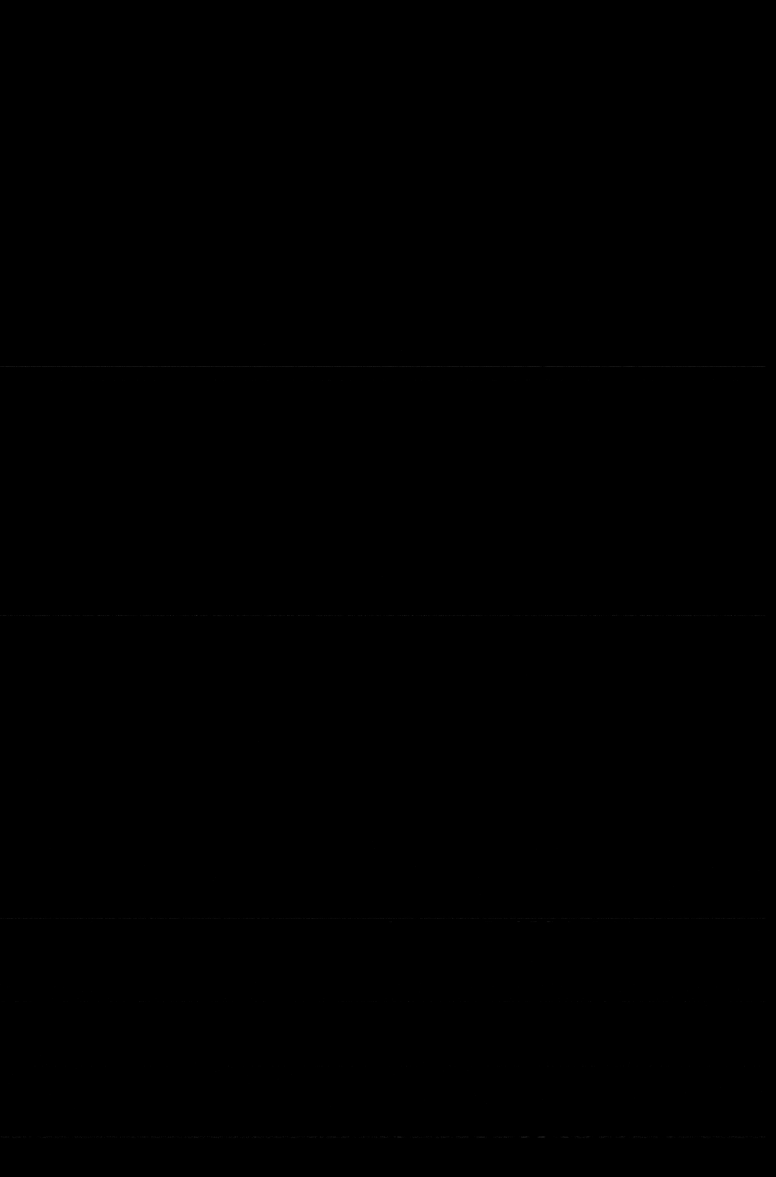

# Bull

I AM NOT SPENDING MORE THAN A DECADE IN JAIL.
Not even to get rid of Pop. I can't do it. I guess that makes me
a real turd. I guess I deserve the beatings coming my way. I
reach down and cup my balls. Yeah, they're still there. I've got
balls. It's just that my balls are only good for punching dorks
in the back.

But I am not weak. I'm not.

It must be the quiet in here that's making me get all
psychological and shit, but I'm wondering . . . am I a murderer? I've never thought of myself as a person capable of real
murder. I stare over the top of my computer, watching kids

silently walk through the library, and I almost say out loud, *So, could I really have shot Pop? As in dead. Blood-gushing, brain-splattering dead?* I could've always closed my eyes when I pulled the trigger. Yeah, I wouldn't have seen the mess, but I would have known what I did. In a complete dick kind of way, my heart would've known.

I reach up and rub my skull with both hands. I wish I could just freaking disappear right now because my head is clogged up with dirt and muck and shit.

Two girls walk by the table, whispering about what bikini will make their boobs look better, and a thought smacks me right in the forehead: School is out in four days; summer is here. Maybe I'll just spend the whole summer working at Salvy—bump my hours to the max—and stay the hell out of Pop's way. I only have two more years at home and then I'm out of here. Two more years. Of beatings.

I can't do it. I can't take two more years of his shit. I don't know what to do. And I have to get to work.

**INJURY NOTED**

K. M. Walton

# Victor

MY MOTHER PICKS ME UP FROM SCHOOL ON THE
second-to-last day of school. She has taken the day off from
her job as the vice president of a bank so she can get ready
for Europe. She says she needs my help lifting things into her
SUV. What she could possibly need my help lifting is a mystery to me. I don't ask. I just do as I'm told.

On the way out of town, we sit at the light by the Salvation
Army building, and she gasps.

"Oh my God, there he is—the animal that tried to kill me."

I look out my window. Bull Mastrick is unpacking some
old guy's trunk.

"Do you see him, Victor?"

In three seconds a whole series of thoughts fly through my head. It is the weirdest thing. One thought leads to another, then another and another, and before I know it, in, like, light speed, I have this whole new thought.

First I think of how much I have to pee, and then of peeing myself on the playground, which leads me to when Bull shoved my head against the wall at the urinal, which goes to me walking Jazzer when she has to go, which makes me think of my mom calling Bull an animal just now, which makes me wonder who named him Bull, because he *is* an animal and he tried to kill my mom, which makes me laugh, because we both got bullied by the same jerk, and I think that's hilarious. Like I said, it's weird.

And I laugh. At the worst possible moment.

The light is still red. We're sitting there, with Bull no more than fifteen feet from our SUV. He doesn't see us because he's too busy working. But I see him, and I am laughing like I'm being tickled. Which makes me laugh even harder, because my parents have never tickled me. The only person who's ever tickled me was my grandfather, and he died when I was six. I only remember him tickling me once before my mother made a scene and practically accused him of child abuse right there in our living room. I still remember

K. M. Walton

how it felt though, the tickling, and the laughing so hard that my sides hurt.

That's how hard I'm laughing as my mother asks, "Do you see him, Victor?" Her mouth is open and her eyes are wide, as if someone has put a spell on her.

The car behind us honks with a friendly *beep beep*. I'm still hysterical. She's still gaping.

*Honk! Honk!* The car behind us is no longer polite.

Bull looks toward the honking, toward us. He sees me laughing. His face changes from curiosity to anger in no time at all. I know he thinks I'm laughing at him because of where he works. And that here I am, sitting in my mother's $85,000 SUV, while he gets paid to take donations from people who have more money than he'll ever have.

His hand shoots out with a gesture of anger, followed by his other. I'm getting double flipped off.

My mother guns it, and I stop laughing. But I'm still breathing heavy. It takes me a minute or so to calm down. In that minute my mother takes a wild right turn and parks in front of the pet store. And so begins her *moment*.

"I'm calling the doctor when your father gets home, do you hear me? I will not allow my son to be on drugs. I will not! Oh my God, what people will think! What are you taking? Dope? Pills? Let me see your arms. Are you using needles?"

She reaches over and grabs my arm. No tracks. She takes her seat belt off and reaches for my other arm. Drug-free too.

I say with as much composure as I can, "I'm not on drugs, Mother. I promise you."

"Then what is the matter with you? Are you hearing voices? Are voices telling you to do things? I'm still calling the doctor. I won't have you ruin this trip for your father and me with all of this craziness."

"I'm not crazy, Mom."

"Well, what do you call what just happened back there? That monster tried to kill me, and you laugh? How insensitive can you be, Victor? We're talking about my life. Do you think me dying is funny? Is that it? You think it would have been funny if that animal actually *got* me?"

She's crying now.

I don't know what to do. My father always handles my mother, and he's still at work. I ask myself what my father would say to calm her down, but everything sounds too lovey-dovey. So I don't say anything.

I want to tell my mother why I was laughing. That we both had been bullied by the same kid. How Bull had gotten to both of us and he didn't even know it. That we must have big red *X*s on our backs, or it must be in our genes, or something.

But I don't tell her. Because she wouldn't understand. I know she thinks she's better than me, and it would make her so mad if I put us on the same level. It would make her yelling worse. I stare out the window as birds take flight off of the pet store sign, flying up higher and higher into the bright blue sky, and I have to close my eyes. It's too normal, too beautiful to look at.

"Well, you just sit there and be quiet. You've ruined the day, Victor, you selfish, selfish boy." With that, she pulls away from the curb and drives home. We don't speak. I turn my head and pretend to look out the window. But I don't want to see the world, so I squeeze my eyes shut and clench my jaw the entire ten-minute drive. I know if I ease up and release my face, the tears will come. I will not give her the satisfaction of seeing me cry.

I will not.

When we pull into the driveway, she tells me to get out and go up to my room, like I'm five. I get out and she drives away. Thank God.

Jazzer isn't in the window when I get to the door.

# Bull

THAT PRICK IS LUCKY I DIDN'T HAVE MY GUN WHILE he was sitting at the light. Figures his mother is the cow that snapped her fingers at me. I swear, the next time I see him, I'm going to mess him up. Thinks he's better than me with his golf shirts and expensive car—they make me sick.

I'm still pissed when I get home after work. I'm mumbling shit to myself as I triple-lock my bike, when I hear Pop and Uncle Sammy through our kitchen window. They're going at it. Loud enough that I swear some of the bricks are gonna rattle themselves loose from the house. I walk around front and the dad from the apartment underneath us is out on the front porch having a smoke. The dude doesn't speak English—he's from Mexico—which is fine by me, because I'm in no mood to explain what the hell is going on up there. He rolls his eyes at me—the universal language for *What the hell?* I reply with a roll of my eyes. He nods. Best conversation I've ever had.

With clenched fists, I climb the stairs to our apartment. Before I put my hand on the doorknob, I take a deep breath and roll my head around on my shoulders. I'm sure I look like a boxer about to enter the ring. I guess I am.

I hear Pop yell, "You're cleaning this shit up!"

Then Uncle Sammy yells, "Just shut up! Shutupshutup-shutupshutup!"

I hear a loud crash and open the door. The apartment is a disaster. It looks like one of them took every bag out of the closet and shook each of their contents all over the apartment. Crap is everywhere. And I mean *everywhere.* My pop is standing in the kitchen with a beer, and my Uncle Sammy is crawling around the floor throwing linen napkins and old shoes up in the air.

Welcome to the nuthouse.

I know what he's looking for right away. Now it all makes sense. Why I never saw that brown bag before. Uncle Sammy must've tossed it in the closet sometime when I was at school. What he wants is not here. I won't tell either of them that, but it's not here.

My uncle looks up from the floor, sees me, and pounces like a jaguar. I'm jacked up against the wall, and he's got the craziest look in his eyes.

"WHERE IS IT, BULL?"

I play dumb and ask, "Where's what?"

"YOU KNOW WHAT!" he spits out, literally.

He's got me by the shoulders, so my hands are free, and I reach up and wipe my face.

"Where did you put it, Bull?" he asks through clenched teeth.

Pop decides to chime in now. "Just tell him where it is, Bull. Sammy's in some trouble."

I continue playing dumb, so I say forcefully, "I don't know what you guys are talking about! Let me—"

My uncle's palm is on my forehead, and he smashes my head against the wall and gets nose to nose with me. His breath smells like he snacked on roadkill soaked in beer, and he sneers. "I'm. Not. Asking. You. Again."

One good thing about people who are drunk, or on drugs—or, as in Uncle Sammy's case, both—is their lack of judgment. He never expects my knee to fly up into his crotch, but it does. I'm instantly released from his grip. I give him and Pop the finger, then I'm back down the stairs in seconds.

I crash into my mother at the bottom, and she falls on her butt.

K. M. Walton

"What the fuck, Bull? Jesus Christ!" she yells at me.

I don't help her up. I'm completely freaked out. I stand there, my knees shaking, looking over my shoulder at the stairs. The porch is empty; the Mexican dad is gone. My legs are frozen. I look down at her and the stupidest thought comes to me: I wish she was the kind of mom that I could talk to. The kind of mom that would protect me.

She grunts. I watch her roll over on all fours and grab her lit cigarette that landed a foot away. She sways as she stands. She's shitfaced.

I try to walk past her, but she grabs my arm.

"Don't you look where you're going? Why're you rushing around? Where are you going?" she shouts at me, then drags on her cigarette, blowing her smoke at me.

I look at her, with her smudged black eyeliner and greasy hair, and I feel my stomach twist inside.

"I feel sorry for you," I whisper. I am immediately pissed at myself for not shouting those words in her face, that I pussied out and whispered them.

She squints and says, "What did you say, you little shit?"

There's the courage. There it is. It surges through me and I say nice and loud, "I said, 'I feel sorry for you.'"

My mom sways and reaches out for me to steady herself on. I take a step back. She goes down again.

I'm not sure how long this courage will last, so I look down at her and say, "You could've been different. You didn't even try. You're just like him."

Mom pulls herself up using the railing this time, and I'm quietly amazed that her cigarette stayed in her mouth the entire time. Her hand reaches up, grabs the cigarette from her mouth, and throws it at me. It hits me in the chest.

"Don't you tell me . . . don't you tell me tha shit. I gave up everythin' for you," she slurs. Then she screams, "Everything! Everything! Everything!" She continues yelling that one annoying word as she stomps past me and up the stairs.

My body comes back alive. I jump off the porch and run around back. I unlock my bike quick, because I don't know who might come flying out looking for me. I don't think I've ever unlocked those three locks faster.

Riding my bike always clears my head. And my head is full of more shit than a stopped-up toilet right now. Sometimes my bike takes me places I never expect to go, like it just leads me. Cars and houses go by me in a blur and when I look up, I'm in front of school. I sit for a minute and try to think of where I'm going to sleep, because there's no way I'm going back to my apartment—not tonight, anyway.

And it's weird. You know how your brain jumps from one thing to another sometimes? Like a whole bunch of random thoughts that connect real fast? Well, I decide that I'm ditching the last day of school. Then I realize that Dad's postcard is in my locker. So I lock my bike and go inside to get it. And while I'm walking through the halls, I tell myself that I'm never coming back to this school, that I'm running away, which sounds girly, so I change it to: *I'm going to find my father.* I look into my locker and smirk. The postcard is the only thing in here that even matters to me. I grab it and then slam my locker shut.

I'm not sure how I'm going to get to the beach, because I can't ride my bike that far, and then I think I could take the bus there. I look down at my postcard and I wonder if they'd let me bring my bike on the bus. I know I have enough money saved to get me to Ocean City. Which makes me think of the cemetery. So that's where I head next.

And that's where the gun is too.

# Victor

JAZZER IS ASLEEP ON MY BED. IT'S THE FIRST TIME SHE wasn't waiting for me at the window. I ask her what's wrong, and she makes that little squeaky sound, yawns, and goes back to sleep. I tell myself that she's just tired, but my heart knows better.

The phone rings. It's my dad. He wants to know why I made Mom so upset. He tells me I owe her an apology before they leave tomorrow.

"You're leaving *tomorrow*? It's my last day of school."

He tells me that my mother changed the flights last week so she could spend two more days in Paris, shopping. He reminds me how much my mother loves to shop and how she is going to need those extra two days of shopping to relax from all the stress I've put her through.

"What time do you leave?" I ask, completely ignoring his stupid logic.

"Noon. Your mother is flying Nana up from Florida. She'll be there when you get home from school."

"What? Nana? Dad, I'm sixteen. I don't need a babysitter."

"After the scene you caused today, sir, you most certainly need an adult in the house. And you're punished. Remember? We want to make sure you are preparing for school next year. Your mother has made a specific list of assignments she'd like you to accomplish while we're gone."

"God, Nana? I'll end up babysitting *her*. And Mom made a list? Seriously?"

Dad tells me I better drop the attitude, that my mother worked very hard on that list, and I had better thank her before she gets on that plane. And then he tells me I'm ungrateful.

I don't say anything.

"Victor, do *not* get your mother upset again. She'll have a stroke. And then what would we do?"

I know what I'd do, but I stay quiet.

"I'm meeting your mother for dinner. She needs to calm down with a good meal. Don't wait up. We may meet up with another couple. We'll see you in the morning. Good-bye."

"Good-bye, Dad."

I can't believe my nana will be here tomorrow. I haven't seen her in a long time. I also can't believe my mother is dragging her seventy-eight-year-old mother from her beachside condo, making her get on a plane, and flying all the way up here just to watch me. All because my parents don't want to take me with them to Europe as punishment for getting a 2060 on my SAT, which is probably better than any kid in my high school.

It's stupid. My mother is stupid. And selfish. She is a stupid, selfish, empty woman.

I clench my jaw tight and then look over at Jazzer. She's all curled up and looks so peaceful on my bed. Not selfish or stupid. Just peaceful.

# Bull

THERE'S ANOTHER BROWN LUNCH BAG SITTING UP
against the tree in my spot. No one is in the cemetery again.
But I walk around this time, just to be sure.

This time there's a bottle of water, a granola bar, a bag of
Cheetos, and a pear. The water isn't cold, so I figure the bag's
been here awhile. Same note in the same handwriting:

*Enjoy!*

Then I do as it says and I enjoy every bite. It's the first
thing I've eaten all day, and it all tastes so good. Even the

warm bottle of water goes down nicely.

I uncover my box and remove my $376.54, shoving it into my two front pockets. I also retrieve the contents of the old brown shopping bag and tuck the gun into the front of my jeans. I tell myself I'm stupid for not grabbing my backpack or something, but then I stop beating myself up for that. I couldn't have grabbed anything. Not under those circumstances.

I check my back pocket and am somehow relieved that the postcard is still there. I exhale loudly because I really do need a backpack—and my books. I forgot my secret stash of books under the sofa. I have to go back. I won't go in if Uncle Sammy is still there. But I have to take them with me.

I bike back to my neighborhood. I have to shift the gun a few times while I pedal because it feels like it's going to fall out, but I still make good time. For a faster getaway I don't lock my bike, I hide it in the alley behind my street. My mother's car is gone, which means my uncle either took it or Mother of the Year is out driving drunk.

I travel ninjalike from bush to bush along the side of the house, and that's when I see my uncle up the street, yelling at some fat guy. He doesn't see me. I'm glad neither of them are in the apartment. It'll just be Pop, and he'll probably be passed out on the kitchen table by now. I can sneak in, grab my backpack and books, and be outta there before Pop even grunts.

As soon as I open the door, he's on me. Pop's drunk, so I'm faster. I duck a punch, and he falls forward onto his hands and knees. I'm across the room like an arrow and he comes at me again. Pop lands a punch in my gut, a good one. I keel over, and he lets me fall on top of the piles of stuff from the closet.

"You really are a dumbass. You're a stupid dumbass!" he hollers to me. "I swear, if I had Sammy's gun, I'd shoot you myself. Then I'd be rid of you."

I shift just a little bit, so the shoe on the pile will stop stabbing me in the back.

This sets him off. My pop puts his foot on me to hold me down. "Don't you move, you worthless pile of shit. Don't you move."

Something in me snaps.

Oh, I move.

I push his foot off of me, jump up, and reach into the front of my jeans for the gun. I want him to feel fear. I point the gun at him. "Why do you have so much hate in your heart?"

"Because I don't got a heart. That's why. You killed my heart when you came along. You killed my heart."

Then I do the dumbest thing I've ever done. I start crying.

"Go on, why don't you pull the trigger? Kill me too, like you killed my Bonnee."

More blubbering from me.

"You know why you won't? Because you're a worthless boo-hooing pussy." Pop knocks me down with a left hook to my jaw.

I close my eyes and squeeze the trigger.

# Victor

MY PARENTS ARE ALREADY GONE WHEN I WAKE UP, though it's only a quarter of seven. They've left me a note on the kitchen counter.

*Victor,*

*We wanted to get lattes before our long drive to the airport and didn't want to wake you. I'm sure you understand.*

*The car service will drop Nana off between 8–8:30 this morning. So she'll be here when you get home from school. See to it that Jasmine stays out of her bedroom; you know she's allergic.*

*Attached is the list of things I expect you to accomplish while we're away. I've made a drug counseling appointment for you, for when we get back. We'll call you when we land in Paris. See you in two weeks.*

*Mom*

No "*Dear* Victor" or "*Love* Mom." I can't believe they didn't even say good-bye to me. Not even good-bye.

I don't want to go to school. I don't care that it's the last day of my sophomore year. I don't care about anything right now. I feel sick to my stomach, like I might really throw up. I can't believe they left me a note, like I'm the housekeeper.

I walk into the foyer and scream at the top of my lungs, "I'M THEIR SON! THEIR SOOOOOOONNN!" I'm screaming at no one. I expect Jazzer to peek her little head through the slats of the railing to find out why I'm yelling. I don't see her.

I plop down on the steps, and my head falls into my

hands. I yell a few more times. It feels good to yell, cleansing in a weird way, and my heart returns to a regular beat.

I stretch out on the steps and call, "Jazzer, girl, come down here."

I left her sleeping on my pillow, so she's got to be up there. She always comes when I call. But I still don't see her. Maybe my yelling frightened her. Maybe I shut my door.

I hop up and take the stairs two at a time, because based on how my day has gone so far, well, let's just say I have a really bad feeling.

My door is wide open. And Jazzer's curled up on my pillow. I am at her side in two strides. Her eyes are open. *Oh, thank God, she's okay.* I reach down to scoop her up and my hand registers that something isn't right. She's stiff. And cold. And not breathing. Her little body is stuck in a curled-up sleeping position. But her eyes are wide open.

Jazzer's dead.

I carefully put her back on my bed and completely fall apart. Like, unglued. I start throwing whatever I can get my hands on. My alarm clock takes flight. My books and all of the decorative crap my mother put on my dresser go flying. The brass bee (who puts that in their teenage son's room, anyway?) leaves a decent hole in the wall. Dad'll love that.

I keep looking at Jazzer, expecting her to be scared

by my insane behavior. But she is so still. That makes me go for the contents of my drawers. It feels good to throw things and grunt and cry. I decide that throwing the brass bee the was most satisfying because it was heavy. So I scan my room for anything that has some weight to it and grab the cordless phone.

"No one has ever called me on this thing any"—I throw the phone as hard as I can—"WAY!" It shatters into a lot of pieces against the wall, and I feel good.

Next, I go for my bedside lamp. I pick it up and am happy that my mother likes expensive things, because it's solid brass. Out comes the plug, and I wind up and throw it with every bit of strength I have. It, too, leaves a hole in the drywall. Way bigger than the bee's.

I look around my room again. Every surface is empty. I've thrown everything there is to throw. That's when I start to sob. I mean loud sobs. I fall to my knees and just go for it.

After my face is covered in pathetic weakness and the sounds I make deteriorate into whimpers, I know I have nothing left. My arm shakes as I slowly lift it to check my watch. I have cried for an hour. School started a long time ago. And it hits me again: the fact that no one will give a damn that I'm not there today. No one will even notice.

I suddenly have a purpose. I get up and walk to my parents' bathroom. The timing couldn't be better, I tell myself. I hope she hasn't packed what I'm looking for.

I open my mother's medicine cabinet and nod. I scan the shelves and reach for the bottle I want. My hand doesn't tremble when I reach for it. It is as steady as a rock. I give the bottle a shake. Freshly refilled.

"Yes!"

I leave the bottle in the bathroom, go back, and close my bedroom door. I cross the hall and walk back into my parents' bathroom. I close that door too. I want Jazzer as far away as possible from what I'm about to do. But I laugh, because she'll know. We are about to see each other. I read once that animals can talk in heaven. If Jazzer can talk, then I'm about to get a real talking-to.

Back in my parents' bathroom, I pop five pills in my mouth and swallow them down with lukewarm tap water.

Five more.

Five more.

Five more.

I refill the bathroom cup and take five more. I walk back to my room. Lying next to Jazzer seems like a great place to die. She was the only one who ever really loved me, so it seems right.

I sit on the edge of my bed. My stomach grumbles, and I

squish the ultraplush carpet under my feet. It's so soft. I look up to check the time on my alarm clock, but it's in pieces. I look at my watch.

7:53.

My nana will be here soon. I feel guilty that she'll be the one to find me, but at this point, there's nothing I can do. I curl up next to Jazzer. I'm so tired from crying.

I've done it. I've really done it. I've re . . .

# Bull

I WAKE UP IN A HOSPITAL ROOM, WITH THE CURTAIN pulled around my bed. I'm alone. Various beeps and lots of people talking make it impossible for me to go back to sleep. I wonder if my grandfather is alive. We struggled with the gun, I remember that. But he must've knocked me out. I don't remember anything past that punch.

Know this: *I'd* never loaded the gun, never checked to see if the gun was loaded, never even thought that the gun could be loaded. I never went back a step to think about, say, someone's uncle putting a *loaded* gun into a brown paper bag and leaving it in a closet. No, I never thought about that.

I slide my bottom jaw from left to right. Yeah, Pop knocked me out. I've gotta go to the bathroom. I sit up, and that's when I see that I'm all wired up. I still have to go to the bathroom, though, wires or no wires. I go to move my legs, and volcano-hot pain rips through my right thigh.

"What the . . . ?" I yell out. I rip off the blankets, and I'm staring at bandages from just below my knee all the way up to my groin. I try to move again. Bad idea.

"Owwww! What the . . . ?!"

The curtain flies open.

"Easy there, killer. Easy," says a nurse. She's totally hot. Tall and skinny with long brown hair, perfect teeth, and enormous blue eyes.

It dawns on me that I have no shirt on and appear to be wearing a diaper. My eyes bulge, and I pull the blanket over me.

"I've seen it all, trust me. And I do mean *all*."

This doesn't help me feel any better. I pull the blanket to cover more of my bare chest.

"Oh, no, no. I didn't see all of *you*. I mean I've seen—" She cuts herself off and sticks out her hand. "Let's try this again, okay? Hello, William. I'm Ellie."

We shake. No one has called me William since kindergarten, but I like how it sounds.

"Hey. Where's my mom?"

K. M. Walton

This question seems to make Ellie uncomfortable, because she drops her eyes and starts rustling with the papers on her clipboard.

"Ellie, has my grandfather been here?" I figure asking about him in a roundabout way is smarter than flat-out asking her if I killed him.

"Yes, he has. He brought you in here, actually. But I haven't seen him since."

"And my mom? She been here?"

Ellie squeezes her lips together and tells me that my mom *has* been here, but she had to be physically removed because she was drunk. And loud.

Great. Just great.

I ask her where I am, and she tells me I'm in the ER recovering from surgery on my thigh to repair damage from the bullet. And waiting for my official bed to open up. I ask her what happened to me. She seems confused by this question and asks gently, "You don't remember trying to kill yourself?"

I take a second and keep my mouth shut. I want to see if she'll keep talking, because somebody told Ellie a lie, and it wasn't me.

"Your grandfather, he was . . ." She trailed off.

I help her out, "Drunk. My grandfather was drunk, right?"

"Well, yeah. But he was able to tell the police what happened after a cup of black coffee."

I swallow hard. "The police?"

She nods. "Actually, William, there's an officer waiting to talk with you."

"Whatever." The police? Shit. What the hell am I going to tell the police?

"You sure you're up to talking? I think I could stall him a bit longer if you'd like to rest more."

I pause and think that resting sounds a lot better than talking with the cop, but I have to get it over with. "Nah, but thanks. I'll just talk to him."

Two minutes later this supershort black guy pulls back the curtain. "William Mastrick?"

"Uh-huh," I answer from bed. We're practically eye to eye, that's how short he is. Between his 1980s glasses and bad hair, I'm thinking he probably got picked on a crapload when he was a kid and became a cop to take revenge on everyone. Genius move on his part, actually.

"Officer Gill," he says with an outstretched hand.

We shake. He smiles. I shit myself.

"Nothing to worry about, son, so just relax. Okay?"

I nod. Still shitting.

Officer Gill pulls out a small notepad and flips it open.

"Last night your grandfather said you guys were having a fight. Is that right?"

I nod my head in agreement.

"And you attempted suicide?"

My conversation with Ellie's prepped me for this, so I nod my head in agreement again.

"Why don't you go ahead and tell me what happened?" Officer Gill says calmly.

My brain surprisingly kicks into overdrive, and I do some lightning-fast reasoning. If this dude thinks I tried to kill myself, then that had to be what Pop told him. Pop must've left out the part where I aimed the gun *at* him. My fists are balled up under the blankets. I have no idea if what I say will contradict what Pop's already told him. I keep it short and general. I get through my whole story in, like, four sentences.

Officer Gill flips to a new page in his notebook and lifts his eyes to mine. "You never pointed the gun at your grandfather, is that correct?"

I nod.

"Did you try to hurt your grandfather, William?"

I shake my head no.

"I'm going to need a firm answer here, son."

"No, I did not try to hurt my grandfather." Oh my God, I just lied to a police officer.

He clicks his pen and slips it into the spiral spine of his notebook. "Get better." We shake hands again. "You have your whole life ahead of you, kid. Don't blow it."

"Thanks." I think I just got away with pointing a loaded gun at my grandfather. If I had the balls, I'd hug Officer Nerdy and cry on his shoulder.

Ellie breezes back in, all smiley and hot. Apparently I'm puffed up with my genius, because I add a fresh layer of bullshit to my story. I lift my head up as she fluffs my pillows, look her right in the eye, and tell her that my grandfather is a hero for saving my life in my darkest hour. I swear I said, "my darkest hour."

She grabs my hand and squeezes. My stomach flips. She is the hottest girl I've ever talked to, ever. Woman—the hottest *woman*. She's probably in her early twenties, and that makes her a woman.

Ellie says, "Your grandfather *is* a hero, William. Don't you ever forget it. Every day we have is a gift." She slips through the curtain, and I'm alone.

I know what my pop did. I get it. He knows the world of problems, starting with jail time, I'd face if he told anyone I tried to kill him. He made up the perfect story. And I'm sticking with it.

It's the least he could do.

# Victor

I WAKE UP IN THE HOSPITAL. I AM REALLY MAD I WOKE up—like furiously, insanely mad. The curtain is closed, and I am alone. My parents are probably livid that I made them come home early from Europe, and I wonder where they are. I cringe at the thought of facing them, talking to them, and explaining my actions. I also cringe because my stomach and throat hurt badly. I swallow and wince.

Why couldn't it have worked? Why *didn't* it work? I took enough pills, I know I did. Why didn't it work?

The curtain is pulled back, and in walks a young nurse holding a clear plastic shopping bag filled with something gray. She introduces herself as Ellie, my nurse; drops the bag at the end of my bed; and reaches out to shake my hand. As I feel her warm hand around mine, I notice her eyes. They're really blue. And her lips are spectacular.

"So, Victor Konig, do you know your last name means 'king' in German?"

I tried to kill myself and my mother's out there telling people about our name. She is too much.

Ellie is still talking. "Yeah, my dad speaks German, and he used to call my older brother Konig all the time. So when I saw your name on your chart, I laughed because I always thought my dad made that up, you know, to make my brother feel important." She pulls out gray sweatpants and a gray sweatshirt from the bag as she talks. "But I just looked it up online and it's true. Your name really does mean 'King.' Did you know that, Victor?"

I open my mouth to answer her and my throat clamps shut. Cue a coughing fit. An agonizing coughing fit. My stomach and throat explode with raw pain.

Ellie immediately snaps into action. She sits me up and lifts my arms straight up. "Breathe through your nose, Victor." I nod and do as she says and the coughing stops.

She says in a calm voice, "Good, now take a few more deep breaths through your nose. Okay?"

K. M. Walton

As I'm taking my deep breaths, she tells me my stomach and throat will be sore for a few days because I had my stomach pumped. She gently brings my arms down and squeezes my shoulders.

I whisper, "I'm good." So that's why I feel like crap.

"Can you get my parents?" I ask.

Ellie drops her eyes and picks up her clipboard.

I watch her fidget. "My parents aren't here, are they?" I say.

Ellie exhales and says, "No, Victor Konig, your parents aren't here. The doctor spoke with your mother just an hour ago. They landed safely in Paris, so you shouldn't worry about them."

"My parents aren't coming home from their vacation, are they?" I reply flatly.

She purses her full lips, and then Ellie whispers, "No, they're staying in Europe."

"And they know what I've done? You told them what I've done?"

"I did."

I drop my eyes and will myself not to bawl.

"I think you need to rest," Ellie says. "Why don't you get out of that hospital gown and put these on? I think you'll be much more comfortable." She pulls back the curtain to leave and then adds, "Your grandmother was here all day. She brought you in. We sent her home to get some sleep. You should do the same, Victor Konig. I like your name, Victor Konig," she says with a wink.

The curtain falls and I am alone.

I feel sick to my stomach that Nana found me, that I made her feel stress and panic. She didn't deserve to find me. I didn't deserve to be found. Period. I am overwhelmed with guilt—heavy, heavy guilt.

# Bull

NURSE ELLIE, WITH THE PERFECT HEAD, EXPLAINS
that since I tried to kill myself, I have to spend some time in
a psych ward upstairs, so they can monitor me and make sure
I'm not a danger to myself anymore. I'll be talking to some
psychologists and junk, getting three meals a day, and sleeping
in a bed—with sheets, blankets, and a pillow—and be waited
on hand and foot for the next five days. Sign me up.

Some dude wheels my bed through the ER and tells me
his whole life story as we wait for the elevator. Wife's sick,
baby girl's sick, both have the flu, he hasn't slept in two days,
and now he feels sick too. And then he sneezes right on me.

He apologizes over and over in the elevator, and then he sneezes again. There are more apologies before he stops talking altogether. I don't even care. He can sneeze on me all day. I'm headed up to a floor with a warm bed and a scorching hot nurse. Sneeze away, sad man.

I'm rolled into room 714, near the window. Someone else is already in here with their curtain closed. Good. I am in no mood to talk to anyone. Especially some crazy suicidal idiot. I just have to play my cards right, keep my mouth shut, and milk my time here. Then I am out. Off to the shore to find my dad. That's my plan.

My jeans. My $376.54 and my postcard are in my jeans pocket. And have a mini heart attack. I shout to the orderly, "Yo, dude, where are my clothes? The ones I had on when I got here?"

"Oh, yeah. I was supposed to tell you about that. Sorry. When you come to this floor, they hold on to your clothes. You know, for your own safety. Normally they give you gray sweats to wear, but since you just had surgery and all, you'll wear that standard-issue hospital gown you got on. And then they'll give you a robe and slippers up here. Don't worry though; you'll get everything back when you're checked out. Be well, brother."

Whoever is sharing my room with me says, "HA!"

I ignore him, because like I said, I am not in the mood to talk to a suicidal freak right now. I stare at the ceiling. That money better all be there when I get my shit back. No way am I going home after I get out of here. I'm done.

# Victor

SINCE THE REST OF MY BODY IS PARALYZED BY FEAR, I'm impressed that my hand reaches for the nurse call so fast. There is no way! No way in hell am I sharing a room with that cretin. Nurse Ellie is by my side pretty fast.

"What's up, Victor Konig? What can I do for ya?" she says with a big, heart-stopping smile.

I whisper, "I want my room changed, please. I can't stay here."

"Whoa, easy there, big guy. You don't really have a choice. When you take a bottle of pills, you sorta lose some say in stuff. Besides, your parents already faxed their signatures from

Europe. This lovely room is your home for the next five days."
More dazzling smiles.

Then she adds, in a loud whisper, "Why were you whispering?"

I motion Ellie to come closer. She leans over, and I breathe her in before I talk. I'm literally dizzy with how perfect she smells. Like citrus and fresh flowers.

I continue to whisper, but into her ear this time. "I know the kid in that bed. And, well, let's just say we're not friends. I can't stay in this room with him."

Ellie turns her head and proceeds to whisper in *my* ear, "Sorry, Victor Konig, but this floor is small. We only have four double rooms up here, and they're all full. You're going to have to work it out with William."

I sit up as relief washes over me, and keep talking low. "William? Not a kid named Bull?"

"William," she says, "not Bull."

"Oh. I could've sworn . . . whatever, I'm good." I shake my head and laugh quietly.

Ellie breezes out, and I smile at my good fortune.

From behind his curtain, William growls, "It *is* Bull, Victoria."

My smile evaporates, and I start breathing really heavy through my nose. My jaw is clenched. I can't do this. Not with him here. Why didn't those pills just do what they were supposed to do?

I punch the bed and get up. I sit back down on the edge of the bed. I have nowhere to go. I can't leave this stupid hospital. I can't do this. I punch the bed again, and that's when the tears break through. The piece of fabric separating me and Bull is no sound barrier, and I refuse to cry in front of him.

I go into the bathroom and shut the door. Where's the lock? Great, no lock. Then I remember where I am and what I'm here for. Of course there'd be no lock. Bull had better not try to come in here; I swear to God I'd kill him.

I turn the shower on, strip out of my prison sweats, and jump in. I just stand there and let the hot water run down my body. My skin looks ashen in the fluorescent lighting. I hold my arms out in front of me, and they're shaking so badly that I drop them back to my sides. Maybe I could steal more pills from somewhere in the hospital, I could suffocate myself, I could . . .

Oh my God. This is insane. This cannot be real. I can't do this.

I slide down the tile wall until I'm in knees-to-chest on the shower floor, and let it all out—again. I cry as hard as I did when I found Jazzer dead. But this time I cry into my bent elbow, so Bull can't hear me. Of all the people on this whole rotten planet, how could *he* end up being in the bed next to me? It has to be God's way of laughing at me. Or punishing me for trying to kill myself.

I have to get out of here. My nana could get me out; my parents probably gave her permission to act as my legal guardian or some crap like that. I could talk her into anything. I have to get out of here.

Immediately.

# Bull

THAT ASSHOLE IS MY ROOMMATE? ISN'T THAT GREAT?
I hate that douche.

I bet he was trying to get Ellie to get him out of here.
He's probably crying in the bathroom right now, the freak.
Well, they can move me, I don't care. I don't really belong here
anyway.

"William, good day, sir. Have you met Victor yet? It
sounds like he's in the shower. Tomorrow you'll be in group
together, so you can get to know each other then."

I am like a drooling idiot. She's talking, but I can't hear a
word she's saying. I'm staring openmouthed at her eyes. She

probably thinks there's something wrong with me, because her eyebrows are arched and she's smirking.

"William, hey, William . . . are you in there?"

I feel my whole head get hot, so I'm probably red, which is embarrassing. "Sorry. What's cool?" I try to not seem like a real mental patient. "You said something was cool."

She smiles. "I knew you weren't listening to me. You had on the same face that my fiancé makes when I'm telling him what I need help with around the house. I asked if you had met your roommate yet. Victor?"

I blurt out, "You can move me, I don't care. He can have this room all to himself. I'll move." Then I'll look like the hero, and I won't have to be near preppy-asshole boy.

She tells me I'm so sweet for even offering to move, but that there are no other rooms and we'll be just fine in here. She'll be back after dinner to check on me. And would I like help taking a shower after Victor's done? I'd have to be tricky and keep my bum leg out of the water.

Her *question* about taking a shower makes me go red in the face again. The question!

"Nah, I'm good. I'm good." I feel my crotch react, and I am so thankful I'm covered in blankets.

# Victor

I CAN'T STAY IN THE SHOWER ALL NIGHT.

I have to go out there.

I don't want to go out there.

I can't do this.

# Bull

THAT JERK HAS BEEN IN THE SHOWER FOR AGES. His dinner tray probably has icicles hanging off it by now. I'm going to be so pissed if he uses up all the hot water. I press the button, and Ellie asks what I need.

I talk into the plastic box. "That guy's been in the bathroom a long time. Can you get him out of there? I wanna take a shower."

"I'll be there in a few."

I polish off my green Jell-O cubes and the water is still going. I hear a knock on the door and Ellie ask if everything is all right. She knocks harder. "Victor? Are you okay in there?"

The water shuts off.

I hear him shout, "I'm good. Sorry."

She pulls back my curtain. "He'll be out in a sec. You sure you don't need any help in there? It's going to be hard to keep that leg dry."

Oh my God. The thought of her seeing me naked—full-on naked—makes my palms sweat. I wipe my hands on the sheets.

"And you're really not supposed to put too much pressure on your one leg yet. Did Rob show you how to use your crutches?"

I didn't even notice them leaning against the wall. I assume Rob was the sneezy, complaining dude that rolled me in here. "Nope, no info on the crutches. But I'll figure it out."

Ellie smiles and grabs the crutches. "I know you could figure it out, William. But you have stitches and we don't need you falling. Stitches are fragile. Like my heart." She reaches up dramatically and clutches her chest. And winks. She talks as she gets me up to a sitting position. "The bullet went straight through and didn't hit any bone, which is really good for you, but it did do some damage to your thigh muscles. And it means you have *two* spots with stitches: the entrance and the exit wounds. You can't get those wet just yet."

I am doing everything in my power not to bawl, because

moving my leg hurts like shit. Ellie is maneuvering me slow and all, but every inch I move is painful. Maybe I don't need a shower. I stop moving and squeeze my eyes shut.

"You okay?" Ellie asks.

I open my eyes and gaze into hers. Man, she is hot. "I thinkIwanna laybackdown," I mumble.

Ellie nods and says, "Take a breather. You're doing great. And your feet are on the floor."

I grasp the bed with both hands and drop my head. All I want to do is lie back down and fall asleep. For a week. I take a few deep breaths and open my eyes.

"Let's try again. You ready?" she asks in the nicest voice.

"Yeah." Even though I said it, I am *not* ready.

Ellie uses her arms to get me up to standing and then whispers, "Woo-hoo, William. I knew you could do it."

I have an overwhelming urge to hug her. Like squeeze her so tight that she'd lose her breath. Instead I just nod and say, "Yeah."

She adjusts the crutches to my height and shows me the basics. I laugh out loud as she crutches across the room, making her legs fly up like a little kid. "Sorry," she says. "Do *not* do that."

"I won't." And then she makes me go back and forth a few times on my own. I turn around to head back, and I get really light-headed and stumble into the wall. She's by my side before I have time to panic, and she leads me back to my bed. I swear it takes me, like, ten hours to lie down again.

With her hands on her hips, Ellie says, "Shower in the morning?"

"Yeah."

I fall asleep with some pretty filthy scenarios running around in my head.

# Victor

I COME OUT OF THE BATHROOM, AND BULL'S SIDE
of the room is dark. I can hear him snoring. My jaw unclenches
as relief runs through my veins. I lift the plastic lid off my
dinner plate and touch the meatball. It's like ice. I chug the
chocolate milk and slurp the green cubes of Jell-O. The Jell-O
feels soothing on my sore throat as it slides down. I push the
rolling cart away and lay back on my bed.

The clock on the wall says it's eight. I wonder what my
parents are doing right now. What fancy French food sits in
their stomachs? In my gut, the gelatinous cubes sit with the
weight of lead, and I feel nauseous.

I run to the bathroom with my hand over my mouth.

Shamrock-green vomit paints the toilet. I slump back on my butt and knock my head against the wall behind me.

Over and over again.

# Bull

I STRETCH AND LOOK OUT THE WINDOW. THE SUN is shining. I can't believe I slept the whole night. Those pain meds kicked my ass. I go to move my leg and the pain is a fierce stab. "Shit!" I yell. I pant a few times to stop the stars in my eyes and throw my head back on my pillow. The room is quiet, and I strain to listen for a reaction from Victoria.

I hear the shower going. Toolbag's in the bathroom again.

My curtain is pulled open and a new nurse says, "Good morning." She points to her name tag and says, "Agnes." If there is a polar opposite of Ellie, this woman is it. Old, really tall, and chubby.

Agnes the nurse says, all serious, "Ellie said you'd need help in the shower. Let's get the process going, shall we? You've got group in an hour."

"No, no, I'm good," I say. My balls just shriveled up at the thought of me and Agnes alone in the bathroom together.

"Suit yourself."

All of a sudden, behind her, Victor's curtain whips closed and I hear him mutter, "It's all yours."

Agnes turns around and asks Victor through the curtain if he's dressed yet. He says yes.

She pulls his curtain open, and there we are. All three of us. One suicidal loser, one linebacker nurse, and me.

# Victor

THERE HE IS.

Neither of us says a word. I am trying to burn holes in his face with my eyes, and he looks like he wants to rip me into tiny pieces.

I break the stare and ask the gigantic nurse, "Where's Ellie?"

"Home." She points to her name tag. "Agnes," she says flatly. Agnes claps once and deadpans, "Okay, boys. Victor, eat your breakfast. And William, you need your shower. Group's in an hour."

I sit down on my bed and lift the lid of my breakfast tray. Gray oatmeal. I'm not hungry.

"Where are my shoes?"

"Probably had laces in 'em, so we keep 'em. For your safety. Don't sweat it, kid; every patient up here's wearing the slippers." Agnes gives me a strained smile. It seriously looks like she doesn't know how to smile.

I don't smile back.

She must sense my annoyance because she says, "Listen up, kid, everyone wears the same thing. Same sweats, same slippers."

"I'd like to speak to my grandmother," I tell Agnes.

"Not possible right now." She puts her hands on her hips, and I swear all she needs is the helmet and pads and someone to yell, "Hut!" Agnes clears her throat and says, "When you're in here, you need to focus on you, so you can get your thinking healthy again. We don't allow contact with family until the fourth day. It's our policy. So let's all just relax and get ready for group. Shall we?"

"I'm fine now. I made a mistake. It was an . . . an . . . accident," I stammer, trying to convince nurse Agnes that my suicide attempt was a silly mix-up.

She pulls my curtain closed and speaks in a very calm voice. "We both know it wasn't an accident, Victor. No one *accidentally* swallows an entire bottle of his mother's prescription sleeping pills. Two, three maybe. But twenty-five pills?

You should know something, Victor: You're here under an involuntary commitment, which means until decided otherwise by the doctor, you'll be here, in this room, in these sweats, for treatment for a minimum of five days. Are we clear?"

I don't want to cry in front of her. In fact, I'd rather shove the handle of my plastic spoon into my eye. But I can't seem to control myself. I'm not blubbering, but there are definitely tears streaming down my face. I know if I open my mouth to talk, I'll make some kind of crying sound. It's bad enough Agnes is seeing me cry, but I would let someone chop my arm off and eat it before I let Bull Mastrick see or hear me cry.

*I can't do this. I can't do this. I can't do this. I can't do this. . . .*
It keeps rolling through my head. And rolling.

# Bull

EVEN THOUGH AGNES TALKED LOW, I STILL OVER-
heard what he did. Twenty-five sleeping pills? And he thinks
they're letting him outta here? Yeah, right. He *needs* group.

I do my best to maneuver myself into a sitting position,
which isn't easy. My leg is still throbbing and really stiff. I have
two really big bandages over where the bullet went in and then
out. I hope I can get them wet.

My crutches are leaned up against the closet, which is next
to the window. Since Agnes is occupied, I'm going to have to
hop once or twice to get my hands on them. It takes me, like,
five minutes just to swivel my feet out of bed and onto the

floor. I grit my teeth as jagged slices of pain shoot through my leg with each move.

Both feet are on the floor when I hear Agnes leave.

Using my good leg, I hop once, twice, pull one crutch under each arm, and begin my short trek to the bathroom. I hope there are towels in there, because it would suck not to have a towel. Victor's curtain is closed, but I wouldn't ask him about the towel situation anyway.

I'm good on these babies. I make it to the bathroom pretty fast and nod a few times when I see the towel, soap, shampoo, toothpaste . . . the works. It feels so good to take a hot shower. A really hot shower. The hot water in my apartment always ran out, especially if the people below us got up first, which they seemingly always did, probably just to tick us off. I think I've taken maybe three really hot showers in my life. And even with one leg hanging out, this hot shower is the best hot shower I've ever taken. No Pop pounding on the door. No mold on the walls. Even though the holes in my leg are starting to burn, it is still a perfect shower.

I don't want the shower to end. I know it has to because group starts soon, and I still have to eat breakfast. I figure I've been in here, like, a half hour. I turn off the water and reach for my towel.

I should've gotten Agnes's help. When I go to maneuver myself and bring my bad leg into the shower stall, my good leg gives out and I'm falling, like in cartoon slow motion. I know this landing is going to hurt like shit.

It does.

# Victor

I HEAR BULL YELL THE F-WORD AND THEN A BUNCH
of other angry words. I'm pretty sure he's fallen. Good. He
deserves it. Let him lie there naked on the floor. I hope he can't
reach the nurse's emergency pull-string, either.

I rub my face. I still remember how much it hurt when he
dug my face into those rocks.

He can rot in there for all I care.

There's more cursing and then, "Aww man, I'm bleeding."
He yells out to me, "YO! Get the nurse, asshole. I fell."

I walk right up to the door and say to him, "Get the nurse
yourself, asshole. I'm going to group."

And I walk out. I leave Bull Mastrick bleeding on the bathroom floor. I don't tell nurse Agnes, either, on purpose.

I'm pretty sure I've just guaranteed my own death, which is fine by me, because I don't want to live anymore anyway. And he'd spend some time in jail for killing me.

That would make me happy.

# Bull

I SCREAM FOR AGNES, FOR ANYONE, AT THE TOP OF my lungs, but I don't scream for long. I guess nurses are trained to listen for idiots falling in the shower. I am facedown and ass-up when the bathroom door opens. I'm sprawled right across the floor. So, yeah, Agnes ends up seeing me naked anyway. I don't really care because of all the blood; I swear, it looks like Freddy or Jason left me for dead. When Agnes gets me back up to standing, she tells me the stitches popped open on the back of my thigh.

She hands me my crutches, and as I try to steady myself, my left arm buckles. "I think I broke my wrist." Great, I'll need someone to wipe my ass, too. Great.

"Sit down on the toilet." And she gingerly helps me sit down, which is not easy because I have to avoid sitting on my bullet wound. "Let me get some more help in here."

Double great. More chicks get to see me naked. Fan-freakin'-tastic.

Agnes comes back with some little gray-haired lady who looks like she could barely lift an infant with ease.

"William, this is Nurse Joan. We're going to get on either side of you and get you back into bed. Any help you can give us would be great."

"Don't look," was all I could say to either of them.

Joan smiles and says, "Relax, son, I've seen every part of a man's body far too many times than I'd like to count. They all look alike, trust me."

This doesn't make me feel any better. It makes me want to punch the wall. I am not supposed to be here, naked on a toilet in a psych ward bathroom, with two holes in my body and a busted wrist. I'm supposed to be at the beach finding my dad. This reality makes me hate my pop so completely that I swear my hate could be weighed and measured and shit.

Agnes, the bruiser, gets under one arm and Joan, the tiny old lady, gets under the other arm. I am glad we made an agreement for "not looking" as I'm half carried, half hopping naked across the room.

K. M. Walton

They get me covered up, and Joan says she's going to call the doctor because I'm going to need to be restitched and I'll need an X-ray of my wrist. So it's just naked me and Agnes.

"See? You should've let me help you. Now you're going to miss group."

"Bummer."

# Victor

GROUP STARTS AND BULL DOESN'T SHOW. FOR SOME
stupid reason I feel guilty. Why, I don't know, but I do. I am,
on the other hand, completely relieved that I don't have to
speak in front of him. I don't plan on saying one word anyway,
but I'm still happy he isn't in the room.

It's a pretty plain room, as rooms go. Baby blue carpeting, cream walls with nothing on them, and two windows
with the blinds down. There are no lamps or sofas. Just one
round coffee table in the center with plastic orange chairs
surrounding it. My mother would call the room cold. She
knows all about cold.

However, there are six other kids in the room, four girls and two guys. After I sit down there are two empty seats, one right next to me. As nonchalantly as I can, I check everyone out. We really are all dressed in the same sweatsuit and slippers.

Directly across from me is this beautiful girl with blond curly hair and humongous, captivating brown eyes. Before I can look away, she mouths, "Hi," to me. And like in the movies, I look to my right and left to see if someone else is saying hi back to her. I look at her, and she's smirking with her eyebrows raised. She mouths, "Hi," again.

Just then the doctor or psychiatrist, or whatever she is, sits down next to me. I stare at her, you know, to see if she looks like she'll be nice. She seems pretty standard. A little on the dorky side, even. Brown curly hair, glasses, no makeup, button-up sweater, long brown skirt, and sneakers. I'm guessing she's in her forties.

"Okay, loverlies, let's get this party started," she says with enthusiasm.

No one else seems to find her use of "loverlies" or the fact that she called this circle of suicidal teenagers a party, odd.

"Victor's joining us today. Welcome, Victor. I'm Lisa, and I'm the therapist running this group."

I nod my head as my hello. I'm not saying anything. That seems to be fine with her and with the rest of the group.

Lisa starts right in. "Okay, Lacey, yesterday you were sharing about your mom, and how you feel invisible when she's with her new boyfriend. How about you start us off this morning?"

The girl to my left pulls a rubber band off of her wrist and shakes back her long blond hair; she twists it into one of those sloppy ponytails all the popular girls at my school wear. Then she kicks her slippers off and pulls her bare feet up onto the chair, wrapping her arms around her legs, and takes a few really dramatic breaths. It's like she's warming up for a big performance or something.

"Yeah, it pretty much makes me sick, I swear. She acts like I don't exist when he's around. I could be shot between the eyes, and she wouldn't notice. I mean, my mother doesn't even really know this guy, and besides, he's a fat slob. Sorry, Brian," Lacey says.

She's obviously apologizing to the fat guy across from me. He's huge.

"S'okay." Brian shrugs.

Therapist Lisa says, "Now, Brian, why do you think it's okay for Lacey to use the words 'fat slob'?"

He shifts in his chair. "Well, I really don't care. She wasn't calling *me* that, even though I'm sure every person in this circle thinks I am a fat slob. But she wasn't talking about me.

It wouldn't matter anyway . . . been called it a freakin' million times. Don't care," he says. And he shrugs again.

"I'm sorry, Brian. That was ice cold, ice cold . . . like iceberg cold. I make *myself* sick sometimes, I swear," Lacey says. She scrunches her face in obvious embarrassment before she puts her head down onto her knees.

The circle is quiet for almost twenty seconds. Therapist Lisa lets the silence in. For not wanting to say a word, I'm finding this silence rather uncomfortable. I shift in my chair and the curly-haired girl catches my eye again. She yawns dramatically, and I give her a tiny smile. I don't want any of these kids thinking I'm making light of their situations. That's the last thing I need. Then Brian talks again.

"You all think I like weighing four hundred and seven pounds? 'Cause I don't. You think I like my face? 'Cause I don't. And I really don't like that both of my parents are whales. So's my sister. You should see us all get out of our van. People stare. Little kids point. *I* make myself sick too, Lacey."

I study Brian and feel pretty sorry for him. He's a heavy guy. As in, I'm kind of shocked they even had his size sweatsuit here. And even if he dropped two hundred pounds, he'd still have tiny eyes that are set way too close together, a big nose, and messed up teeth. I'm observing, not judging. I'd *never* want to make him feel bad about himself; I just don't

have it in me. Another observation? He's clearly in a lot of pain right now.

Therapist Lisa weighs in. "Is that why you tried to end your life, Brian?"

"I wanted to die because I was sick of being stared at, and laughed at, called horrible names. Sick of no one in school ever seeing me. Me, not the weight—me. I was sick of my parents filling every cabinet, fridge shelf, and freezer—we have two freezers—with food. Tons and tons and tons of food. I couldn't get away from it. I was sick of me and how I look. That's why I wanted to end my life."

"How do you feel now? Right now?" Lisa asks him.

"Hungry," he says with a smile.

That gets a laugh from the circle. Even I smile. Brian's whole face changes when he smiles. He looks genuinely happy when he smiles, and not so broken.

Lacey waves her hand; she has something to say. "I see you, Brian. Not the weight. I see *you*, I swear. Wanna know what I see?"

He nods.

She puts her feet back on the floor and leans forward a bit. "Well, I've only been in here with you for three days, but this place is sort of intense, so we probably get to know more about one another in one day than kids at school would get to

know about us in, like, a hundred years, right?" She pulls up her sleeves and smiles. "The Brian I see is funny. And I don't mean funny-looking, I swear. I mean, you are seriously funny. You make us laugh every day. I see the Brian who really loves his mom and dad, but wants them to stop making it so hard for him to lose weight. I see the Brian who has really pretty green eyes that twinkle when he smiles. I see the Brian who is going to get out of here and tell his parents where to shove their bad food, and the Brian who's going to live for, like, forever. I swear."

Lisa tells Lacey that what she did was very brave, and thanks her for being so honest with Brian. Brian is openly crying and the kid on the other side of him hands him a box of tissues. That's when I notice that there are boxes of tissues on the table in the middle of the circle. Like, five boxes. I swear.

# Bull

THEY HAVE TO RESTITCH MY EXIT WOUND. THAT'S real fun. After my X-ray and the news that my stupid wrist is broken in two places, they try to put me back in the ER to wait for my cast. But I kinda throw a fit, like a two-year-old with a dirty diaper. I don't want to go back there. It's too loud. Too crazy.

The doctor throws her hands up and shakes her head. As she jogs away, she yells over her shoulder to the new dude wheeling my bed around, "Just take him back up. I'll send Carl up there when I can."

The new dude says to me, "I don't blame you. This place

is wild. There was a bad car accident, that's why Dr. Pearse just gave in like that. She's usually a lot feistier. You lucked out."

On the elevator ride back up, I laugh out loud to myself. I actually *want* to go back to the psych ward, with the psychos. Funny.

Ellie's there when the doors slide open, with her arms crossed. "Causing trouble, William?" She smiles.

I smirk.

Ellie chuckles. "Yeah, that's what I thought." She excuses the orderly and wheels my bed down the hall. "I'm gone for a few hours and you fall apart on me."

"What can I say? Trouble follows me."

I see that my room is empty, so I ask Ellie if my mom has called. Or my pop. I don't know why I care, or why it feels like a kick in the nuts when they haven't. I'm allowed to call them on the fourth day, though. Which I guess Ellie thinks will make me feel better, but doesn't. I'm not calling them.

I ask her to close my curtain; I want nothing to do with *Dick*toria. Like that? That's his new name. I can't believe the dick left me on the floor.

Well, I can kinda believe it, but I still hate his rich guts.

I stare at the sun out the window as Dr. Carl puts the cast on my arm. The guy is a man of few words, and I'm thankful, because his breath stinks. Then I'm casted and alone again.

A snack arrives, and I have trouble not smiling like a clown. It's a blueberry muffin, chocolate pudding, and Sprite. It's food. Food that's delivered on a tray. And I love every bite.

With my good arm I scrape every single bit of pudding out of the plastic container. Then I start thinking about my dad for some reason. All I know is his name. Steve Gallagher. I don't know what he looks like, how tall he is, what kind of car he drives. Heck, I don't even know what he does for a living. All I know is that he wanted me gone before I was born. *Get rid of it,* was what he wrote on the postcard. I should've used the stupid computers in school to look him up online. I could've gotten an address or phone number. Something. Maybe I can get online here. Maybe it'll be easy to find him.

I roll my eyes.

He probably won't want anything to do with me. He might not even know I exist. Knowing my stupid mother, she didn't even tell him she had me.

All this makes me want to throw up my muffin.

Speaking of puke, Dicktoria never comes back to eat.

K. M. Walton

# Victor

AFTER GROUP ENDS, THE OTHERS WALK ACROSS THE hall to what they call the common room. Lacey calls out to me as I start to head back to my room, "Hey, Victor, come hang out with us."

I don't know why I turn around and walk toward the room, but I do. It is really freaking me out that I do. Maybe I don't actually want to spend the night sitting three feet away from Bull Mastrick, wishing I had the guts to take his stupid crutches and just beat him till he begged me to stop.

Walking in that room means I have to talk to these kids. Am I ready for that? Apparently I am, because I'm sitting on the sofa.

The common room looks like a hospital waiting room, just with couches instead of plastic chairs. It has a TV, shelves with boxes of games, and a table with chairs where the two guys go start playing cards. Three of the girls spread out on the sofas, and then there's me on one by myself. The other girl with the long black hair and the sour look on her face sits in the corner, facing the window, and writes in a notebook. I guess it's her journal or something.

One of the sofa girls asks me, "So, what did you do? Wait, let me guess: the car. You used the car, right?"

"No way, he's pills. He's definitely pills," the blond, curly-haired girl says. She is seriously the hottest girl to ever talk to me.

I am solidly stunned that she even spoke to me at all. "Yeah, pills," I say to her. I wonder how she knows this, but I'm afraid to ask her.

The not-Brian guy turns around from the card table and says, "Parents are real assholes, you get bullied at school, never been laid, got no friends. Am I right?"

"Pretty much," I say, trying to figure out if they're making fun of me or just showing off their creepy knowledge of suicide. Great, I can't believe I just admitted to five strangers and the hottest girl alive that I'm a virgin. Genius.

Nurse Ellie peeks her head into the common room and announces that some snacks are ready next door. I'm glad she's back. Everyone jumps up and darts out, and Ellie comes in and tells me that once patients are up to it they eat everything in the dining room. That it is so much nicer to sit at a table and eat. Which I think I'll agree with.

She says it helps build friendships, too. That, I can't see happening.

Ellie walks me into the dining room and announces, "Bon appétit." The dining room is a small room with one long rectangular table surrounded by eight plastic orange chairs. In the middle of the table sits a tray of blueberry muffins and another tray of bananas. A whole bunch of sodas and juices are scattered in between the trays. I take the empty seat next to Brian. The hot girl is all the way at the other end.

The table is set with a white tablecloth and a centerpiece of fresh flowers. I can see the hospital has attempted to make this feel like home, except they've clearly failed on some crucial points:

1. The tablecloth has faint stains.
2. The flowers are almost dead.

Despite the dirty tablecloth and crunchy flowers, everyone sitting around the table seems surprisingly normal.

Not me. *I* am stained and almost dead.

Most of the kids talk to each other and I just listen. I swallow a few bites of blueberry muffin, and I realize something. It is pretty cool to actually sit at a table with kids my age and not be asked to get up and leave.

Or be sucker punched in the back.

# Bull

I WAKE WITH A START. AND I YELP. I JERKED MY freaking leg. The room is still dark on Victor's side and I wonder where the hell he's been all day. Then I say out loud, "Who gives a shit?"

I'm trying to get comfortable when I notice a brown lunch bag sitting on my nightstand. It's rolled up exactly like the two I found at the cemetery. I freak out a little bit and start looking around, half expecting someone to jump out of my closet or pull back the curtain. After a minute or so I'm pretty sure I'm alone. I unroll the bag. A plastic bottle of apple juice, a wrapped danish, another granola bar, and an orange. And another Post-it.

*Enjoy, son.*
*The poem is from when I was*
*a young dad.*
*—Frank, the caretaker*

*P.S. Your bike is safe.*

So, it *was* the lawnmower guy. I didn't think he ever saw me, though. And how did he find me here? I never said one word to the guy. It's weird, but in a good way. I reach back into the bag and stuck to the bottom is an old newspaper clipping with a poem typed on it.

Just a Little Peace

Many children know pain
heartbreak
disappointment
at the hands
of those meant to love them

Many children lie in darkness
broken
crumpled
longing for whispers
that everything will be okay

Dreaming
dreaming
dreaming

K. M. Walton

about survival
retribution
just a little peace

Children want to be loved
cherished
without conditions
restrictions
limitations
or boundaries

A child's spirit is a fragile thing
a hollow egg
delicate and easy to shatter

Some wait to be filled
with direction
hope

Some wait for no one
they fill
themselves
up

I reread the Post-it and the P.S. smacks me right in the face. I think: *My bike!* I never locked it, and well, we all know what crazy crap happened next.

What did this Frank mean by "safe"? Did he mean he has my bike? How am I supposed to find it when I don't even know where he lives? Then I think that he must've spoken to one of the nurses. He was in my room, so he had to have talked to someone, right?

I use the nurse call box and ask Ellie who dropped off the brown bag of snacks. She tells me his name is Frank and that she's surprised I'm asking her this question, because Frank gave her the impression that the two of us were close, personal friends. I don't want to get old Frank in trouble. So I tell Ellie that it must be my new pain medications playing with my head because, yes, I know Frank from the cemetery, like, really well. And yeah, we are close, personal friends. And thank you, Ellie. I add that last part so she won't think I'm lying to her super-hot-nurse-self.

Now it's just me, the bag of food, the Post-it, and the poem. I may read a lot, but I've never read a poem before. Well, that's sort of a lie. I've been read stuff that rhymes, like Dr. Seuss and junk, but I've never read a real poem. Ever.

I read it once, then turn the clipping over to see if there's another one on the back. There isn't. I read it again. And again. And again.

And then I start crying. Yeah, I'm serious. I'm crying.

# Victor

AFTER THE SNACK WE'RE ALLOWED TO GO BACK TO
the common room, where my interrogation lasts for another
ten minutes. I guess everyone didn't want to ask "those questions" at the table with the other nurses hanging around. Jenny,
the other girl who was sitting on the sofa, tucks her brown
hair behind her ears and changes the conversation. Thank
God. She says to the hot, curly-blond-haired girl, "Nikole, tell
everyone your story. It's just so freaking sad."

*Nikole,* I repeat in my mind. I let the name sway and spin
through my head as she talks. I say it over and over again. I
think I hear her say she got here two days ago.

*Nikole. Nikole. Nikole.*

It's the most beautiful name I've ever heard. Brian's cough clears my thoughts, and I pay attention.

Nikole is saying, "Some drunk driver swerved and then a third car smashed into Greg's side of the car."

Lacey takes Nikole's hand into hers and squeezes. "Why are some people so effing irresponsible? I swear."

Nikole says to Lacey, "I don't know. I loved him. And he loved me. We applied to the same colleges and—" She chokes out a cry.

Greg was her *boyfriend.*

No one says anything for a while, and the only sound is Nikole sniffling. Then she gets herself together and says, "So I took a handful of pills from my mother's medicine cabinet, left a note, and went to bed."

Even though Nikole is beautiful, she somehow seems gray and dull—like someone peeled off the shiny layer of her outer shell. I wish I could've seen her happy.

She told us that when she woke up in her bed the day after taking the pills, she was mad. Her mom found the note while Nikole was in the shower. Her mother then proceeded to freak out, call this place, and get her in treatment within two hours.

Jenny says, "I still can't believe you didn't need to get pumped."

Nikole shrugs. "I didn't take enough of any of the pills. I just grabbed a few out of every bottle I could find. The intake guy said I was lucky and if I'd taken, like, four more Valiums, I would've either been in a coma or dead."

I hear Notebook Girl go, "Psh," from the chair in the corner. She doesn't lift her head or anything. She's still writing, her face hidden by her hair.

None of the other kids appear to have heard the "Psh" because they don't acknowledge the girl at all. Conversation kind of lulls, and pretty soon, one by one, the room empties out—even the girl in the corner leaves.

It's just me and Nikole now.

As she speaks, I am doing everything in my power to respond with the appropriate facial expressions, which is probably backfiring and making me look like a complete weirdo. This whole talk-to-people-like-you're-a-regular-person thing is as foreign to me as my parents' love and acceptance. I tell my brain to shut up and just listen to her.

She tells me she had the weirdest dream last night: Greg came to her and kept reassuring her she would be all right. It made her want to live again.

Really, I can't believe such a beautiful girl is talking to me, looking me in the eyes, and waiting for me to react to what she is saying. *Looking* at me. *Seeing* me.

"I knew you were pills," she says, and smiles.

I feel my mouth try to form the shape of a smile, but I worry it looks like I just farted or something.

"What?" Nikole says, still smiling. "What's that face for?"

I shrug and shake my head.

"So, do you have any brothers or sisters?" she asks.

"No, just me."

"You're lucky. I have three sisters, and I sometimes wish it was just me. You know, so that I could be who I am and not what they want me to be."

"Yeah," I say and look at the floor. I have no idea how to keep a conversation going.

She gets up from her couch and plops down next to me. "Did you ever wish for something, Victor?" she asks.

My breath is caught in my throat. She's got tears in her eyes, which makes mine instantly fill up too. I make my lips tight so that I don't full-on cry, because I know that would be the lamest thing I could do right now. I nod. She nods with me, raises her hand, and puts it on my cheek. Now the tears are dripping from my eye sockets and down my face. She takes her thumb and wipes them away without saying a word. To be honest, her *eyes* are telling me what I've desperately wanted to hear my whole life: *You're okay just the way you are.*

The funny thing is, *I* want to fix *her*.

I feel more bonded to Nikole after a few hours together than I do to both of my parents combined. And they've known me for sixteen years.

One of the nurses comes in, smiles, and says, "Just doing my rounds." I quickly pull myself together. Nikole says she's going to read in her room.

"Sure," I say.

We both get up, even though I have nowhere to go. And in the hallway Nikole turns one way and I turn the other. I watch her walk toward her room. She turns around, walks back to me, and whispers in my ear, "Your dreams *are* going to come true, Victor. I can feel it." Then she kisses my cheek.

Again I watch her walk toward her room, but this time I can feel the blood surge in my sweatpants. I go directly into the bathroom and brush my teeth, which I understand is a peculiar reaction. I am in there for two reasons:

1. I don't want to have any interaction with Bull right now.
2. I need my boner to go away, and figure brushing my teeth is a pretty regular and mindless thing to do until it does.

Bull's curtain is closed when I sit on my bed. I swear I hear a sniffle and a small choke. Then I hear it again. It's very soft, but it is definitely the same sound.

Bull Mastrick is crying.

I wish I had a secret video camera. I could record this so I could show it to the whole cafeteria. Then maybe, just maybe, he would never punch the chocolate milk out of me again.

I imagine smiling as the whole school watches him cry like a little girl. I smile big and wide.

Then I hear the crying sound again, this time not so low. And Bull whispers, "Shit."

K. M. Walton

# Bull

I CAN'T BELIEVE DICKTORIA IS BACK AND I HAVEN'T pulled my crap together. He knows I'll end his life if he tells anyone about this. Maybe he didn't hear me. Whatever, I'll kill him if he talks.

I think I've read the poem at least ten times. Each time I read it, fresh tears roll down my stupid face. Every single line of that poem hurts. Each line is like a dog bite in the ass. Why would Frank give it to me? Was he *trying* to make my life even more depressing?

Why would a guy I've never even met drop off snacks like I'm going on some dumb field trip? And why shove this poem in there? He must be ticked off that I keep sneaking into his damn cemetery when I'm not supposed to be there. He's just as much of an asshole as Dicktoria.

Why did he call me "son"? I'm not his kid. Maybe he's one of those creeps who like . . .

Whatever.

I'm not crying anymore, which is good because I hate crying almost as much as I hate getting pounded on by Pop.

My thigh hurts, my wrist hurts, my stomach hurts, my eyes hurt, and yeah, I'll admit it, my heart hurts. I'm out.

# Victor

BULL STOPS CURSING AND CRYING AND IT IS QUIET.
I lie back on my bed even though it's the middle of the day.
What the hell else do I have to do? Silence always makes my
mind go deep; I usually try to make it come up for air and
get out of the murky depths. But I let it go this time. You
think I'd be reliving the whole Nikole moment, but no, I
sink down . . . down . . . down . . . down. . . .

My parents leave me home from our family vacation so I
can get perfect SAT scores. My parents leave me behind. On
purpose. Not like in *Home Alone*. It was a real decision—and
I know it made them happy. This makes me sick and angry.

I start sweating. I turn over on my stomach and breathe rage into my pillow. I'm almost sure I hate my parents.

I struggle for a few minutes to conjure one good thing about them. Memories invade my dive into blackness, pulling me closer to the surface.

My mom is brilliant with wound care. Not that I got hurt a lot, but she would always swoop in with her first aid kit and bandage me up. Like when I fell off of my bike in fourth grade and ripped my knee wide open. It was so bad you could see bone. Did she get all woozy and call for my father? No, she calmly held the cut closed with one hand and worked the first aid kit with the other. But on the way to the emergency room, I distinctly remember her ruining the moment with, "Now, Victor, if that bandage isn't sufficient to stop your bleeding, please tell me immediately. I don't want your blood ruining the seats in my car. Do you understand me?"

Tenderness.

But I have this other memory that I'm not entirely sure I haven't imagined. I was four, and I had woken up in the middle of the night because of a bad thunderstorm. I remember walking into my parents' bedroom and tapping my mother awake. She had smiled, pulled the covers back, and patted the bed. I had crawled into my mother's warm arms, and she'd kissed the back of my head. I'd laid still and remember telling myself not to move because I didn't want to be told to go back to my own bed, alone. I had felt perfect. I had felt safe. I had felt loved.

I don't think it really happened. My mother isn't capable of such compassion. I think I cooked it up just to make my mom seem human. More like an actual mom, you know?

I've never asked my mother if it was real, and I never will, because I know she'd tell me I was being ridiculous or pathetic or ludicrous. She'd say I must've made it up.

And then I'd be left with nothing.

# Bull

I WAKE UP AND IT'S MORNING. I SLEPT FROM yesterday afternoon (after my boo-hoo session) through the whole freaking night. I stretch carefully because my leg is wicked stiff.

My breakfast tray is sitting on the rolling table next to me. It smells like pancakes, which makes me think of my mother.

When I was in second grade, she went on this kick and decided to become the kind of mom who cooks for her kid. Up until then, cooking meant opening a can of soup or smearing butter on white bread. Dinner served.

But then she decided to go to the store and buy a whole

bunch of cooking crap. Like pancake mix and eggs and real potatoes and a whole chicken and rice. I'd never seen a whole raw chicken in my entire life, and I'll never forget the three of us just staring at it on the counter like it was shrink-wrapped alien poop. It was that weird-looking. At eight years old I knew my mother wouldn't know what to do with that dead bird, and I was right. It sat in our fridge until it started to stink. One day I came home from school, and I could smell it all the way from the bottom of the stairs. My pop made me wrestle it into the trash and smacked me in the back of my head because I didn't get it out fast enough.

My mom did try to make pancakes, though. We didn't have any milk or cooking oil, just pancake mix and eggs. So the pancakes sort of tasted like floury scrambled eggs. She also forgot to buy syrup. But it was food, so I ate it.

I got a good ass-kicking from Pop that morning. He said I was making faces when I ate the pancakes. I never made a face. He was the one making faces. I ended up with a serious welt right in the middle of my back, which made sitting at my school desk a real treat. I couldn't lean back against my chair for two weeks.

Ahhhh, pancakes.

I lift the plastic lid off the hospital plate and smile; it *is* pancakes. And sausage. I don't even bother with the spoon;

I eat everything with my one good hand. My plate is clear in less than two minutes. I move on to my fruit cup and down it. Then finish up with my orange juice. All gone.

I don't hear anything from Dicktoria's side and I wonder if he's still sleeping. Ellie breezes in and tells me that when I'm feeling up to it, I'm welcome to eat breakfast with the rest of the kids in the cafeteria down the hall. She tells me that's where Victor is. Like I care where he is. Group is in an hour, and she'd like me to go today. I tell her I'm not up to it. She tells me I don't really have a choice, with a huge, stomach-melting smile.

"Up and at 'em, Sir William. I'm not letting you shower alone today."

I raise my eyebrows.

She raises her eyebrows back at me and smiles. "You know what I mean!" she says. "Now let's get you up. Lean on me."

I guess I don't have a choice, because she's already helping me sit up. I give her a half smile as my stomach rolls my breakfast around, mixing it nicely with the terrifying reality of her seeing me naked. I instantly feel nauseous and I wince.

Ellie stops and says soothingly, "William, relax, okay. I'm a nurse and this is my job. You have nothing to be embarrassed about. Now just let me help you."

I close my eyes, take a deep breath, do as she says, and the next thing I know, I'm in a wheelchair on my way to the bathroom. She says she put a special chair in there for me so that I can sit during my shower.

"I am going to be right on the other side of the door to help you back into the wheelchair. And no, I won't look."

Ellie helps me out of my gown and gets me situated. I'm naked on my shower chair. One hundred percent naked. My body realizes this in like two seconds and sends blood to my crotch just to further embarrass me. She never takes her eyes off mine.

I think I love her.

# Victor

BREAKFAST ISN'T THAT BAD—PANCAKES AND SAUSAGE. The only annoying thing is trying to eat it all with a spoon while you're trying to look cool in front of Nikole. I end up losing a piece of sausage midmeal as it rebels against the spoon and flies across the table. This makes Nikole laugh. Her laugh is contagious, and the whole table ends up laughing.

At first I don't know how to react, so I immediately shrink into self-protection mode. But after a few seconds I realize that these people are laughing *with* Nikole and not *at* me. She jabs me and then leans her head against my shoulder, all while she is giggling.

I like when people laugh *with* me and not *at* me.

"Did you see how far that sucker went?"

Suddenly I laugh, hard. My body seems to wake up from the inside out as it shakes and makes noise. To be honest, I really can't remember the last time I laughed like this. Maybe when I was a kid? I don't know. But right now laughing makes me feel alive.

It ends up being a great breakfast.

Therapist Lisa floats in and announces that group will be early today, like in an hour, but I don't hear the reason why. I'm lost in the happiness pulsing through my veins. The hospital staff begins to clear the table, and I wish I could freeze time. I want people to be still so I can fully appreciate this feeling. Nikole stands up and I get up too.

Ellie appears in the doorway and says, "Hey, guys, the cleaning staff is in the common room. You'll have to hang in your rooms till group. Sorry about that."

We all head back to our rooms, which doesn't take long. The ward itself (that's what everyone here calls it) is only a small wing on one floor of the hospital with four bedrooms, a small nurses' station, dining room, common room, group therapy room, and a doctor's office—which has been dark and locked since I've been here—and that's it.

I'm still smiling about the sausage when I realize I'm going to have to face Bull. I replay the events of yesterday. Me leaving him on the bathroom floor. Me calling him an asshole. I am thankful he is injured because if he wasn't . . . well, let's just say it would be a bloodbath. Why does he have to be my roommate? Of all the people in the whole damn world, why do I have to have *him*?

I do not want to walk in there. I can't walk in there. Fear grabs hold of one of my ankles and terror grabs the other. I'm frozen in the hallway. Literally frozen. I can't move. I can't go in there.

"Hey, Victor Konig," Ellie says, waving me into my room.

Bull is wet-headed and now wearing his own gray sweats, sitting in his wheelchair by his bed.

"Okay now, gentlemen. I am only one woman. So Victor, I need you to do me a favor," she says. I must look stunned or stupid because she singsongs, "Helloooooo? Anybody in there? Victor?"

I nod my head while my heartbeat gongs in my ears. I think I know what she is going to ask me to do, and I won't do it.

"Good, you're with us. Now, Victor, I'm going to need you to wheel your roommate around for me. You know, to the cafeteria and group."

I knew it. I knew it. I knew she was going to ask me that.

# Bull

I AM AN IDIOT. A WEAK-ARMED IDIOT. WHY DID I have to break the wrist on my good arm? Why? Because I'm an idiot, that's why. I know I'd have the strength to wheel myself around if I had broken my other arm. But no, now Dicktoria has to wheel me around like we're boyfriends. Maybe one of the other kids in group will do it for me, but they're probably all dorks like him. Boo-hoo, nobody likes me, waaaaahhh.

Stupid wrist. He is beyond lucky that I'm stuck in this effing wheelchair or I'd kick his ass when he gets out of the shower.

I'm all fired up.

Bull speaks. "Ellie, I got it. I'm fine. I don't need help."

Ellie huffs with a smile. "Oh, William, you've got it, do you? How do you think you're going to wheel yourself around with a broken wrist?"

With a smirk on his face, Bull raises his good arm up and shakes it.

"One arm? You think you can maneuver this wheelchair with one arm? Try it," she says.

Bull rolls about two feet and then he stops. His face screws up in anger. I've seen that look before.

Ellie turns to me and says, "So, Victor Konig, you game?" Her eyes literally sparkle like when the sun hits the ocean. She's that hot. My brain shouts, *NO, NO, NO, NO, NO, NO, NO, I will NOT wheel that turd around!!!* But I feel my mouth move, and I hear my words betray me. "I guess," I mumble.

"Good! Thanks, King Victor. You guys have group in forty-five minutes," she says, and then she's gone.

I don't say a word to him. I grab the fresh towel from the foot of my bed and head directly into the bathroom.

As I stand in the steaming hot shower I openly insult myself.

*You idiot. You freakin', freakin' idiot. You stupid, freakin' idiot.*

And out of the blue I start reciting that poem in my head.

*Many children know pain, heartbreak, disappointment at the hands of those who are meant to love them.*

I stop and laugh. Me, Bull Mastrick, reciting poetry. *That* is a real shocker.

I have the poem almost memorized, but I can't remember the ending. I reach over and grab it off of my nightstand. I read it again.

My face is getting hot. What is the matter with me? Why would I read it now? He is going to be out of the shower soon. Wouldn't that be such a cute scene—me crying in my wheelchair?

Hell no.

I want to rip the paper to shreds. But I stop. I punch the arm of my wheelchair with my good fist. I can't do it.

The poem is true. That poem is my life. Well, the first three stanzas of it, anyway. Heartbreak? Yeah, check. Pain? Pop has his PhD in that shit. Broken and crumpled? I feel like those words and everything they stand for are what's pumping through my veins. Not blood.

But the strange part? It's the rest of the poem that made me bawl last night, especially the "hollow egg" part. And the word "fragile." I realized that if I counted up the times in my shitty life where I've felt like a fragile egg, well, I'm pretty sure it would be in the hundreds. No kid should have to feel breakable.

What I should've had was the part about being loved without conditions and limitations and shit. It's what any kid wants. What every kid deserves.

I only got the first three stanzas, and that blows.

A-hole's out of the shower and pushing me down the hall without a word. Fine by me. Even though I almost lost it again back there in our room, I can't give up this opportunity.

"You ever ignore me like that again, DICKtoria, and I'll knock your ass out," I say. I tilt my head back to look at him and instead get a view up his nose. He acts like he doesn't hear me and looks straight ahead. He's such a chickenshit.

"I know you hear me," I say to his chin.

He does more ignoring. I can't really knock him out while sitting in this wheelchair, but we have stopped moving, so I put my head back down. I'm now in a small circle. All eyes are on me. Right away I say a mental, *Thank you, Ellie*, as I see that we are all dressed in sweats and slippers. If I had to face these people with my ass hanging out of a hospital gown, I think I'd crap myself.

I don't smile at anyone. I just stare at them individually. I can tell this makes the fat guy uncomfortable because he scrunches his face and then moves in his seat. The girl with the long, greasy black hair lifts her eyes from some notebook she's scribbling in and starts blinking. A lot. Some of the girls smile, but the other dude in the circle smirks at me. I don't like him already.

A dorky lady starts talking. "Good morning, my loverlies, let's get this party started." All eyes turn to her. "We have another new group member. Everyone, this is William. William, this is everyone."

I do nothing but stare. The lady breaks my angry stare by saying, "Welcome, William. I'm Lisa, and I'll be the therapist running your group sessions. Anytime you'd like to talk or join in, you don't need permission. Same goes for you, Victor. All right, yesterday we left off with Brian and Lacey sharing a very important moment. Brian? Lacey? Would you like to start us off?"

A girl, Lacey, nods and then talks.

"I still feel really bad that I said 'fat slob' in front of Brian," she says, "I mean, I couldn't stop thinking about it. I feel like I should've been more, like, aware or something. I just feel really bad that I hurt you, Brian. I swear."

I know the fat dude's name now.

He says, "Yeah, I know you feel bad. I could tell. I'm not saying it doesn't hurt every time I hear crap like that, but I'm used to it. You said some nice stuff yesterday, though, and that made me sleep really good. I didn't have any nightmares last night. Which is pretty cool."

Lisa tells him this is a big breakthrough for him and that he needs to think about why that is. She tells him to write down what he comes up with and bring it to group tomorrow. He says he will.

I look around the circle and notice this hot girl with curly blond hair silently mouthing words to Dicktoria, and he's smiling and whispering back to her.

Lisa sees this too. "Nikole, Victor, you know the rules. No sidebar conversations in group. Would either of you like to share?"

Nikole smiles and says, "I'm sorry, Lisa. It's just that Victor and I really want to hear the new guy's story." Victor looks like he just swallowed an ice pick.

"And why is that, Nikole?" Lisa says.

"Well, he's the only one in a wheelchair, and we think he probably has an interesting story. You know, how he ended up in here. That's all."

The whole circle of people turns to me.

I know my face is red; I can feel it. There is no way in hell I'm talking to this group of freaks. None of them would understand what I've been through. I can just tell. They can just die for all I care.

I want to kill Victor Konig.

# Victor

NIKOLE IS THE COOLEST PERSON I WILL EVER KNOW. She has no fear. Well, actually, she has no idea there's a monster sitting across from her, because if she did, she would've never put him on the spot like this. Not Bull Mastrick. No way. But she doesn't know anything about him, and she wants to hear his story.

She spontaneously orchestrated the whole thing as soon as I sat down next to her in group. She made fun of his scowling stare and said she was going to make him talk. I smiled back at her and let her go. I can't believe she said "*we* think he probably has an interesting story." We. Not I. We. As in me and her. For once I've got this whole group of people around me who laugh *with* me, talk *to* me; he wouldn't do anything in front of them.

Bull doesn't say anything. Lisa jumps in. "Nikole, Victor, thank you for trying to include William. William, would you like to share your story with us?"

He shakes his head no.

"When you're ready. Only when you're ready," Lisa says calmly. I watch Bull's chest collapse as he releases a breath. I want Lisa to push him. I want him to squirm in that wheelchair. I want him to crack and shatter into little pieces so the custodian sweeps him up and dumps him in with the rest of the hospital trash.

But Lisa redirects the group and gets Jenny to talk about her cheating boyfriend. We hear all about it, every single dramatic detail. Lots of tissues are used during Jenny's time, and with Lisa's guidance, she ends up concluding that ultimately, she's afraid to leave and go back out into the real world and face him. The other girls chime in with advice and supportive statements of how she can do it, and by the end I think she feels pretty good about herself, but who knows.

I feel jealous of her. I wish *I* could open up and just dump my entire hideous life into the center of the circle for everyone to dissect and give me advice—but Bull's here.

K. M. Walton

Group ends on a positive note. The girls hug Jenny and promise to keep in touch, and we all head into the common room, everyone except Jenny and Lacey. They head to their room arm in arm. I hear Lacey say, "Well, at least you don't have anything to pack."

I'm sitting on the one sofa next to Nikole, carefully watching her tuck her hair behind her ear and thinking it's incredibly sexy, when Brian stands in front of me and says, "Hey, dude, aren't you supposed to wheel that new guy around?"

"Crap," I say. I totally forgot about Bull.

I am about to walk back into the group therapy room, but I stop because Bull is talking to Lisa. She must've gotten him to open up after we all left. And I think, *She is* good, because we've only been gone for, like, two minutes. I overhear hear him say that his grandfather tried to stop him from shooting himself, they struggled with the gun, it went off, and he got shot in the leg. He says his grandfather is a real hero. His back is to me, and I wish I could see his face, because I have never heard him use that tone of voice. It sounds human—and I would really like to see if his face looks human too.

But I never will. Lisa pats Bull on the shoulder and gets up to turn his wheelchair around, and I panic. I jog back down to the common room, plop on the couch next to Nikole, and try to act like I've been there the whole time. When Bull is wheeled in by Lisa, he's got his regular I'm-a-total-shithead face on that I know well. He really does make me sick.

"You forgot your roommate, Victor," Lisa says with a smile.

"Yeah," I say, "I did."

"Bye, everyone, I'm off," she says. "Group'll be regular time tomorrow. Enjoy your afternoon off, loverlies."

Bull looks uncomfortable.

Andrew, the nonfat guy, asks him how he got all banged up. He starts to tell the room the same story I just overheard him tell Lisa. Nikole is also talking to me, but I can only hear Bull.

"Wow, so your grandfather found you with the gun? That's crazy," Andrew says, kind of in awe.

"Mmm-hmm, crazy," he says.

Lacey chimes in. "I read that ninety percent of all suicides attempted by guns are successful, I swear. You must've really wanted out."

"Yeah, I guess," he says. He shifts in his wheelchair and drops his eyes like he wishes this conversation would go away.

"What got you so bummed out?" Lacey asks.

He shrugs his shoulders.

"Well, we've all got reasons. None of us are here by accident. I just wanted to hear yours, that's all."

I feel a tap on my shoulder. "Victor? Over here," Nikole says. I turn and look at her. "Have you even heard a word I've said?" she asks with a fake scowl mixed with a smile.

I shake my head and try to look apologetic. I tell her I'm sorry and then want to punch myself in the face for ignoring a girl. A girl who took me by the hand and pulled me to the side because she wanted to talk to me. What a moron. No wonder I've never had a girlfriend.

She motions to where Bull is sitting. "Why do you care about him anyway? He seems like a jerk to me."

"I don't care about him, believe me. And he is a jerk; you have no idea."

"That sucks that you have to room with him. At least you only have to be in your room to sleep."

"Yeah, I know," I say. God, I wish I could tell her how much her conversation means to me. That when she looks me right in the eye, it makes my organs quiver. Every single one.

"You have nice eyes," she says.

I'm not kidding. She says those words, in that precise order, directly *to* me. I am rendered mute.

Nikole smiles at me. "I'm serious. You do. They're the best brown. They kind of remind me of caramel. Sort of."

I have never, as long as I've been alive, had anyone give me a compliment about how I look. I swallow hard and hope to God my face doesn't misinterpret my utter amazement for confusion or something worse.

She smiles again. And her whole face lights up. She looks so pretty that I'm not sure a professional poet would be able to capture it with words.

"I mean it," she says, and then pokes me in the shoulder. "You should have more confidence."

I nod and roll my eyes. Me with confidence. The thought almost makes me laugh out loud.

"My mother is always telling me and my sisters that 'no one can hold a candle to her girls.' We all just laugh and stuff, but you know what she's doing? Building our confidence. Making us feel special. So, Victor . . ." Her voice trails off. She reaches over and grabs my hand. "No one can hold a candle to you, either."

I feel light-headed.

"Thank you," is all I can come up with. I wish I had the balls to reach over and kiss her, but I don't. I wish I could make her swoon and giggle and do all the things I've seen the popular girls do whenever they talk to the popular guys. I drop my eyes. I've got zero game.

A loud bang makes Nikole and I jump, and our hands release. Andrew is punching the table like a maniac. Then he jumps up and lunges at Bull. And the first thing I think is: I hope he knocks him out.

# Bull

"EASY, DUDE!" I SHOUT, AND PUSH ANDREW BACK
with my good arm. "Don't take it out on me! I didn't make
you run over that dog! Easy!" I look around to see if anyone's
coming to my rescue. Nope. Where are the hospital staff?

Andrew runs his fingers through his hair and sits down.
He's panting. I don't say a word. Right before his meltdown,
he was getting into his "story" with me. He's definitely got
anger issues. He's bat-shit crazy.

Andrew's dad left when he was seven and never came back;
his Mom remarried a control freak who criticizes every move
he makes. They have a second kid, who is the golden boy.

Makes Andrew feel worthless and stupid every single day. No wonder he's pissed off at life.

Then his girlfriend dumped him, and he got cut from the basketball team because his grades were in the crapper, so he decided he was going to drive his car off the quarry cliff near his house. How about that one? Said he was going to drive right through the fence—gun it, you know? Except he took some pills before he left his house and was sort of high, and he ran over his neighbor's dog. Right in front of the dog's family. They were all outside waiting for the school bus. He said the little boy was holding his dog in his arms and wailing. Andrew said he hears the crying every single night just as he's about to fall asleep.

That's when he started pounding the table, screaming, "I can't even get my own suicide right! I can't even get that right! I can't even get that right!"

And then he came at me.

He's talking to me again.

"Hey, I'm sorry. I . . . I . . . I don't know why I did that. Sometimes I—oh, I don't know. I'm sorry."

"Whatever. We're good," I tell him. If he pulled that shit out in the real world, I would've handed him his ass on a platter. But I'm stuck in this wheelchair in the crazy joint. I let him slide.

I look around the room and everyone's eyes are bulging out of their heads. The fat guy looks like he's gonna pass out. Dicktoria and his little girlfriend are looking too. The girl with the long, black, greasy hair is squinting at me, like it was my fault. I squint back at her. She gives me the finger. I pucker my lips and send her an air-kiss. Then she gives me two fingers, one on each hand, side by side. I shake my head at her. If she were a cougar, I think she'd pounce on me and rip me apart. She puts her head down and goes back to writing in her dumb book. I turn away and leave her to her anger. She's obviously whacked.

Andrew says, "Can I talk to you for a minute?"

I try to judge if he'll go ballistic again. He looks pretty calm, so I relax. I shrug my shoulders. "Sure. Just don't come at me again, all right?"

"I won't. I swear to God."

"Good," I say. I look around and no one is paying attention to us anymore. Even the double-fingered, greasy-haired maniac has her back to us. But I figure if I have to, I could always knock him out with my cast.

Andrew whispers, "Do you still have the gun?"

I squeeze my eyebrows together. "What?"

He leans in, rests his elbow on the arm of my wheelchair, and whispers again, "The gun? Do you still have it?"

# Victor

NO ONE HAS FIGURED OUT THAT BULL AND I KNOW each other. That I hate every cell in his body. I wonder when it will all come out.

The common room empties. I see Brian talking with nurse Agnes in the hallway, and she looks very concerned. She calls Andrew over, and Brian walks away. Andrew and Agnes walk down the hall, away from the cafeteria. I guess Brian told her about Andrew's freak-out.

Jenny and Lacey come out of their room, and Jenny's all dressed in regular clothes. Brian joins them, and they walk toward Nikole and me.

# Victor

NO ONE HAS FIGURED OUT THAT BULL AND I KNOW each other. That I hate every cell in his body. I wonder when it will all come out.

The common room empties. I see Brian talking with nurse Agnes in the hallway, and she looks very concerned. She calls Andrew over, and Brian walks away. Andrew and Agnes walk down the hall, away from the cafeteria. I guess Brian told her about Andrew's freak-out.

Jenny and Lacey come out of their room, and Jenny's all dressed in regular clothes. Brian joins them, and they walk toward Nikole and me.

I have an inner battle raging inside. I squeeze the arm of my wheelchair with my good hand and grit my teeth. I look up at him.

"Just don't do it, Andrew." I wish I could give this kid a hundred reasons why he shouldn't finish himself off, but I don't know him well enough. Shit, I barely know myself.

Andrew stares at the floor and I can tell that he's about to cry. And yeah, I *really* can't handle that. He nods a few times and then walks away.

Ellie floats in and announces lunch is in the cafeteria. She gets behind my wheelchair and pushes me. But out in the hallway she starts wheeling me toward my room. She says I have a surprise waiting for me.

I have had enough surprises today to last me a freaking lifetime.

I shake my head. "No."

"Shit," Andrew says. He sits back hard in his chair and intentionally bangs his head against the wall.

Now I'm confused. "Why?"

He exhales really loudly, but doesn't say a word.

"Dude, why?" I ask.

"Nothing. Don't worry about it. I'll figure it out."

"Figure what out?" What is this guy talking about?

Andrew closes his eyes in deep thought. The guy is weird. But at least he's not flipping out anymore. I just let it go, and we both sit there for a few minutes. The babble and laughter of everyone else fills the quiet. I'm pretty sure I know what he wants the gun for—probably to finish off the job he messed up with the whole running-over-the-dog thing.

He still wants to die.

That makes me feel sad for him, and I don't feel sad for other people. As in *never*. I don't know what to do with this feeling. It's kind of like a boulder in my brain. I look down at my lap and exhale.

Without lifting my eyes to Andrew's, I say, "Don't do it." I can't look at him, because me feeling sad for him might show on my face. I can't handle him seeing that.

Andrew stands up and mumbles, "Why not? Why the hell not?"

K. M. Walton

I look around the room and everyone's eyes are bulging out of their heads. The fat guy looks like he's gonna pass out. Dicktoria and his little girlfriend are looking too. The girl with the long, black, greasy hair is squinting at me, like it was my fault. I squint back at her. She gives me the finger. I pucker my lips and send her an air-kiss. Then she gives me two fingers, one on each hand, side by side. I shake my head at her. If she were a cougar, I think she'd pounce on me and rip me apart. She puts her head down and goes back to writing in her dumb book. I turn away and leave her to her anger. She's obviously whacked.

Andrew says, "Can I talk to you for a minute?"

I try to judge if he'll go ballistic again. He looks pretty calm, so I relax. I shrug my shoulders. "Sure. Just don't come at me again, all right?"

"I won't. I swear to God."

"Good," I say. I look around and no one is paying attention to us anymore. Even the double-fingered, greasy-haired maniac has her back to us. But I figure if I have to, I could always knock him out with my cast.

Andrew whispers, "Do you still have the gun?"

I squeeze my eyebrows together. "What?"

He leans in, rests his elbow on the arm of my wheelchair, and whispers again, "The gun? Do you still have it?"

"What's that about?" Jenny asks us.

"Andrew flipped out," Nikole says. Then she turns to Brian. "Why did you tell on him, Brian? That wasn't cool."

Jenny makes a shocked face. "You told on him? You shouldn't have done that."

"I didn't tell *on* him." With a soft voice Brian adds, "I guess I'm worried *about* him, that's all."

"Well, Agnes'll probably put him in solitary now. She's a bitch. You ever been in solitary, Brian?" Jenny asks.

"No."

"I have. I was only in there for, like, three hours, and I thought I was going to lose my mind. All I did was get mad and overturn my breakfast tray. I didn't punch anything or almost attack someone. I don't know. They say it's for your own protection, but I think it's just so they don't have to deal with you. He'll be on some good meds, though." Jenny puffs her cheeks out and exhales. "Maybe I *am* ready to get the hell out of here, you know?"

No-nonsense Agnes asks us to clear the hallway, so we all say another good-bye to Jenny before heading to the dining room. The light is on in the doctor's office for the first time since I've been here. Agnes pushes open the door, and Jenny walks in. I'm sure I will never see her again.

What's left of the afternoon is spent zoning out in the

common room watching the dumbest '80s movie ever. Agnes comes in and announces that dinner's ready. It feels like home. We all eat our pieces of fried chicken and spoon mashed potatoes into our mouths like robots. For, like, five minutes there's just chewing and breathing. No one talks. Five minutes is a pretty long time to sit in silence. Not for me, though. I can go days without saying a word. Except for when I talk to Jazzer.

Jazzer . . .

Why did I have to think of her now? In front of all these people? I feel my face getting hot. My spoon slips out of my hand and bounces across the table.

I jump up and get out of there as fast as I possibly can. I leave my fried chicken, and I love fried chicken. My uptight mother never serves it. She calls it common and messy and poor-people food. I always ate it whenever they served it at school and loved every messy, common bite.

I run into my room. Stupidest idea ever. *He's* in there, all propped up in his bed, eating his fried chicken with one hand. I want to smash his tray against the wall.

I turn to leave and bump into Nikole, hard enough that she falls backward and lands on her butt. I throw my head back and exhale.

She picks herself up before I have a chance to offer my hand.

K. M. Walton

"Geez, Victor, what's the matter? You ran out of there like your dog just died."

I start laughing. Then I start crying. Nikole must think I've lost my mind. I have nowhere to go. I can't go into my own room. I can't go back into the cafeteria. I panic. I bury my face in my hands and slide down the wall behind me. I try to cry as quietly as I can, but it gets too hard and I choke out weird noises. Nikole sits down next to me, rests her head on my shoulder, and takes my hand.

She doesn't say a word. She doesn't really have to. Her actions are speaking to me—like, shouting to me, actually. *I'm here for you, Victor! It's going to be okay, Victor! Let it all out, Victor! I'm here.* I marvel at this superpower.

Agnes and Ellie just leave us be in the hallway, which is great. After a few minutes Nikole must sense that I'm calming down. She pulls her head off my shoulder; right away, I wish she hadn't. Her head felt warm. It felt right.

"You okay?" she asks, squeezing my hand.

"I don't know," I admit. "I'm not sure."

"Why did you freak out?"

I tell her all about Jazzer and thinking of her in the cafeteria. I tell her how Jazzer used to squeak when she slept and that she was the best listener and a bunch of other cool things about her. And then I drop my head and tell her that

Jazzer had been the only thing that kept me from killing myself.

Nikole puts her beautiful head back on my shoulder and says, "Jazzer was your angel."

She squeezes my hand again, lifts her head, and we are eye to eye.

"I'm thinking that what I said to you, about looking like your dog just died, was meant to be. Think about it. That is beyond weird, Victor. You were *supposed* to get this out. Don't you see?"

I'm not convinced, but I muster up an "I guess" to keep the conversation going.

Nikole starts giggling. I think it makes her look even more adorable. But a terrible, familiar feeling creeps in. She's laughing at me. Oh crap, she's laughing at me. I can't take her laughing at me.

She nudges me and says, "Oh come on, don't you think it's sort of funny? I mean, you fly out of the cafeteria because you're *thinking* about your dog dying and right after that I say, 'You ran out of there as if your dog just died.' That's . . . funny. That's funny, Victor. It is."

Her eyebrows are raised, waiting for my reaction.

I start laughing. It *is* funny.

"Victor, we're going to be okay. For some reason, I just know it," she says to me.

I get my laughing under control and say, "I wish I knew it."

"Was that your wish? To make it?" she asks.

"No, that wasn't it."

Her eyes, her lips, her cheeks, her hair—*all* of her is staring at me. I've never had someone look at me this way. My face goes red. At least I'm not crying this time.

She smiles at me. "I think I know your wish."

I shake my head. "No, no you don't. Believe me."

# Bull

I GOT A NEW BROWN BAG FROM FRANK. IT HAS TWO granola bars, an apple, and lemonade. No danish this time. There's another Post-it note, though.

*Enjoy! Hope you are getting better in there. Your bike is missing you. So am I. —Frank P.S. You can keep the poem.*

I keep reading the "So am I" over and over again. He doesn't even know me. How could he miss me? But I like that he misses me. Which is weird because I've never met the guy. But he misses me. That's cool.

Dicktoria flies in, stares at me for a second, and then runs out like a weirdo. I hear a muffled collision and then an *oomph*. I think he knocked his girlfriend down in the hallway. Smooth. I overhear Nikole ask him what's wrong and then him say something about a dog dying. Then I hear him lose it. I wish I were out there to see him because I'd laugh right in his face. She lets him go for a few minutes and then gets him talking. He tells her that his dog was the only thing in the world that really loved him, understood him, saw him. He tells her how she used to wait for him in the window every day after school. And how he found her all curled up on his bed with her eyes open, dead.

I'm jealous that he can tell that girl how he feels. I'm jealous that he had a dog that loved him. I'm jealous that he had a bed.

But mostly, I feel bad for him. And that scares the shit out of me.

# Victor

I AM SITTING ACROSS FROM THE PSYCHIATRIST IN HIS office. Ellie had seen me and Nikole sitting in the hallway. She'd told me I had my appointment with the doctor in five minutes.

And here I am.

I have the hardest time looking into his eyes. He has really long, black eyebrows with gray hairs mixed in. It's like his eyebrows are waving at me, saying, *Look up here. Look up here.* They are the longest and weirdest eyebrows I've ever seen in my life.

His face is odd too. Like the parts don't go together or something. His eyes are really big, but really close together. He has a nose the size of a toddler's, and a small mouth with no visible lips. But he is married. He found someone to love him. After spending two minutes with him I think his wife, whoever she is, must be either blind or deaf. His voice reminds me of breathing, and he is impossible to understand. It's almost like he's talking through me, not to me. I just keep nodding, pretending that I'm getting everything he's saying. I think I hear him say "committed" and I panic.

"Doctor Billings, I'm sorry, can you repeat that?" I ask.

He exhales, obviously annoyed that I stopped his train of thought, and he speaks slowly, pausing between phrases for added emphasis. "I asked . . . if you've had thoughts of suicide . . . since you've been involuntarily committed."

"No," I say.

"Good. Good. And why do you think that is?"

"I don't know." And I really don't. I'm not lying to him.

"Well, I've spoken with your grandmother and your parents. They're very concerned about you, especially your grandmother."

I skip right over my parents and ask about my grandmother. She's the only one I care about at this point. Basically, she's all I have.

"What did my nana say?"

"She just wants you to be okay, and to come home. She wants you to be happy," he tells me.

This actually does make me happy. I wish I could tell her that. I'll have to remember to tell her when I see her. That she made me happy. She'll like that.

"Are they mad at me, my parents?" I ask him. I don't know why I ask him this. I don't know why I even care what they think.

"They're very upset, Victor. You frightened them."

Not enough for them to come home from their vacation, though.

"Are *you* mad at *them*?" he asks me.

I look around his office and think. It's nothing like the psychiatrist offices you see on TV. His desk is small and gunmetal gray. No leather sofas or big plants or piles of books. Just some crappy artwork on the one wall and the same orange plastic chairs as in the cafeteria.

"Are *you* mad at *them*, Victor?" he repeats.

I'm still thinking. Not sure how to answer. Am I mad at my parents? I don't know if "mad" is the right word. I proceed cautiously. "Why are you asking me that?"

He lifts his head and tilts it to the right. And he stares at me. Great, he's waiting for me to talk. I don't want to talk to him. I just met him. I'm not spilling my guts to him. He doesn't know me. Who am I kidding, no one knows me. No one. Well, maybe Nikole, but we just met.

K. M. Walton

What the hell.

"Yes," I say.

"And why is that?" he asks.

"I don't know," I whisper. This is hard.

"Well, you are the only one who would know, son," he says gently. "*I* certainly wouldn't presume to know how *you* feel."

I'm glad he's perked up and not breathe-talking anymore. I can actually understand him now. But I still don't want to answer him. This is way too hard. He's waiting for me to talk again. I can't look at him, so I drop my eyes and focus on my slippers.

"I guess I think it's wrong that they didn't come home from their trip. You know, even after what I did." I stop there. That's pretty big for me. The doctor doesn't say anything. More silence. He probably planned this whole thing: the question, the waiting, the silence. I look up at him, and he's nodding, like he agrees with me. Well, I'm not sure if he agrees with me. I keep going.

"How could they stay there and have fun?"

"That's a good question, Victor. How could they do that?"

He's definitely agreeing with me. This gives me a little confidence, like I'm right, like he's going to call my idiot parents and yell at them. Oh, how I'd like to sit and listen to that.

"I tried to kill myself, and my parents are over in Europe

deciding what chardonnay to have with dinner. My mother is probably shopping all day, filling up their hotel suite with Louis Vuitton bags and Chanel suits, when she should be here at home, filling up her life with me," I say. I start blinking a lot. The tears are trying to get out. I think the blinking is working to hold them in.

"Something in your eye?" he asks.

I suck in some air and tell him I'm fine. I wonder if one of his eyebrow hairs has ever gotten in his eye. Wow, those things are *creatures*.

The doctor asks me how I feel about my parents' actions. Duh, didn't I just tell him that? But he's waiting for me to speak again.

"I feel . . . invisible."

I smile in my hospital bed. Then I snap out of it. That is the dumbest thing I've ever thought of. When I get out of here, I'm going straight to the shore. And if I can't find my dad, well, then I'll live on my own. I can get a job and get a room for cheap in one of those backpacker places. Maybe I'll even go to school, if I feel like it. But I know one thing for sure: I am not going back to my apartment. Ever. Those two can rot in hell for all I care.

Still not sleeping.

I would give anything for a book right now. I'm so desperate, I wouldn't even care if Victor saw me reading. Tomorrow I am definitely asking Ellie to get me a magazine or something to read.

I reach for the poem. This time I focus on the second half of the poem. I like that half.

```
Children want to be loved
cherished
without conditions
restrictions
limitations
or boundaries

A child's spirit is a fragile thing
a hollow egg
delicate and easy to shatter

Some wait to be filled
with direction
hope
```

```
Some wait for no one
they fill
themselves
up
```

I wish my mom and Pop knew about this poem. It probably wouldn't have made a difference, though. They have
big problems. I read the lines over and over again, because I
do want to be loved. Not "Oooh, I love you, you're so hot"
love, just love. Like regular love. I've never thought about this
before. I didn't even know I wanted this.

But I do.

# Victor

IT'S LUNCHTIME ALREADY. AS I WALK BACK FROM THE common room to pick up Bull I realize it's day three, and that means I get to call my nana tomorrow. I really want to hear her voice. I wonder when they'll let me call her. In the morning? Will they make me wait till nighttime? I want to tell her I'm sorry. Sorry that she had to find me. I want her to know that.

This morning was kind of lazy, just a lot of hanging around. Bull didn't want to go to the common room. I overheard him tell Ellie that his leg was aching and that he'd rather have breakfast in bed.

Now I'm sitting on my bed waiting for Bull when he says, "Yo, I'm ready," from his side of the room.

The way he said it makes me want to punch him in the face. Why is he always so damn condescending? *Well guess what, scumbag, what if I'm not ready?! What if I don't want to roll you around here like we're best friends?! What if I'd like to push you and your wheelchair down a flight of stairs? What . . .*

"YO! Did you hear me? I said I'm ready."

I take a really deep breath and clench my jaw. I swear to God I'm going to crush my teeth into tiny pieces. I don't say a word to him. I pull my curtain back, get behind his wheelchair, and push him toward lunch. Ellie had said that he should eat with everyone today even though he's still in a wheelchair, because it's better that way. She said they have a higher table all ready to go for him. Who cares?

I know I don't.

I push Bull into the cafeteria and then let go of the handles. Job done. He's on his own now. The wheelchair rolls a few feet and he puts his good leg down to stop from crashing into his special table.

Nikole is waving me over to the empty seat next to her. Everyone but Andrew is already seated: Lacey, Brian, and Kell. I found out Kell's name this morning. Not from her, she hasn't said a word since I've been here. Nikole told me. Kell's the female version of the old me. Alone, silent, trying to stay invisible. I'm sad for her all of a sudden. And I feel like I want to talk to her, which is crazy because I never want to talk to anyone, ever.

Kell has her head down, playing with her macaroni and cheese. I'm glad she doesn't see me because I've already chickened out. I can't talk to her. I tell Nikole I'm going to get some food. On my way back I see Brian is now sitting with Bull at his "special" table, which is really just a smaller, raised-up version of the table we're all at. Except he doesn't have the tablecloth and dead flowers.

I'm sitting with my tray when Nikole asks me what kind of guy William is, as a roommate.

Do I tell her I know him? Do I tell her he's tortured me since I've been a little kid? Do I tell her he's one of the reasons I tried to kill myself? Do I tell her I hate him more than any other person alive?

I can't dump all that on her. I don't even know her that well.

"I don't know," I reply.

"Well, you live with him, don't you have an opinion of him?" she pushes.

"We don't talk much."

"Oh," she says. "That's kind of weird. Don't you think? I mean, you're like five feet away from him and you guys don't talk?"

"Nope," I say, and pay extra attention to my macaroni and cheese.

Lacey leans in and whispers, "I think he's kinda hot, I swear. I mean, he's all injured and stuff, but he's got those huge green eyes and long eyelashes. I'll bet he'd look even hotter if he let his hair grow out, I swear."

I think I'm going to get sick. *I* swear.

"Anyone who ends up in a wheelchair after a suicide attempt is messed up, seriously. I hope he talks in group today," Nikole says.

I'm beginning to wonder if Nikole thinks Bull's hot too. Why else would she care about his pathetic story? That would send me over the edge, I'm pretty sure. I decide to stop this crap.

"He's a jerk," I say. I want to say that he's a complete asshole, but I don't want to curse in front of girls. My mother might fly back home just to slap me across my "fresh face."

"I thought you said you didn't have an opinion of him. Now all of a sudden he's a jerk? I don't get it," Nikole says.

"Yeah, well, I'm telling you that he's a jerk. That's all. He's a jerk."

I look across the room at him. He's smiling and eating and having a great time over there with Brian. All happy and buddy-buddy, while I'm sitting at a table with girls. God, *loser* runs through my veins. I push my lunch tray away; I've lost my appetite.

Lacey asks, "I wonder how Andrew is? Do you think he'll be in group today?"

I shrug.

In breezes Lisa. Group is in ten minutes, so I guess we'll all find out.

I look over at Kell, and she's got her head down, her long black hair falling over her shoulders, and her hand is going a mile a minute. From where I'm sitting I can't tell if she's drawing or writing. I think she's writing. I wonder what she's writing. What could possibly hold her attention for such long periods of time? I haven't seen her interact with anyone. Well, except for the fingers she gave Bull.

Kell looks up at me and we lock eyes. She breaks the stare in a split second, but it was just enough time for me to see some serious pain in her eyes. A deep blackness.

I can relate.

# Bull

VICTOR HAS TURNED INTO THE DWEEB LADIES' MAN
in the psycho ward. That's funny. He's always with the chicks.
Not me, nah.

At school that kid never said a word to anyone; now
he's making his moves over lunch. Funny. I wonder what
he's talking about over there with those girls. The one girl
keeps looking over at me and smiling, the one who always
says, "I swear." She's not bad-looking, kind of cute. I think
her name's Libby or Lucy or something. Whatever. I don't
want a girlfriend. Can you imagine me taking a girl back to
my apartment?

*Libby, this is my alcoholic grandfather. Better duck, he hits hard. And this here is my mother. Yeah, I know, she looks young. She had me when she was seventeen. Oh, you want something to eat? Well, let's see, how about a piece of moldy bread with . . . yeah, with nothing. Sit down. Oh, careful, that's my bed. Yeah, my bed. This is my bedroom and the living room. Don't mind Pop, he always throws beer cans at me. Pop, don't punch me when my girlfriend's here. Pop! Really, stop punching me! Stop hitting me, you asshole!*

What a date. I'd be the perfect boyfriend.

Not.

Brian seems all right, and he's kind of funny.

"Guess what? I have good news. I added up how much me, my sister, my mom, and my dad weigh, and it is, like, 10,641 pounds less than an elephant," Brian says with a smile.

I'm not sure if I should laugh or not.

"I'm serious. You know how many times I've been called an elephant?" he asks.

I shake my head.

"Probably, like, 10,641 times. But now, whenever some tool calls me an elephant, I can tell him to stick it up his ass, because my whole family put together doesn't weigh as much as *one* elephant. How 'bout that for good news?"

When Brian laughs, I figure it's okay for me to laugh too. So we're both laughing. It feels really good to laugh.

"And I'm getting out of here after group today," Brian says. "Nice."

The therapist lady comes in and tells us group starts in ten minutes. Right away I wonder if Andrew will be there and if the double-finger girl will talk today. She's sitting over there in the corner with her notebook and her pen. I really want to know her deal. I can tell she thinks she's all badass with her dyed jet-black hair and her evil glances, but she doesn't scare me. No one scares me.

I take a piece of broccoli from my lunch tray and wing it across the room. It lands perfectly in her lap. Score.

She flies up, book and pen clattering to the floor, looks around, sees me smiling and waving, and throws it back at me. Nice arm. The broccoli makes it back to me, hitting me in the shoulder. She's giving me the finger—times two again—and then storms toward me.

She leans over and says right in my ear, "I wish the gun worked and you died."

Wow. Nice.

She gives me the twofer again, walks back to grab her notebook and pen, then storms past me and is gone.

I notice two things. One, she has breath that smells like

vanilla. Two, her eyes are the coolest green color I've ever seen. Well, really, I notice three things. I also got a clear view down her shirt when she leaned in. And let's just say she's got a rockin' chest.

Holy shit.

# Victor

TYPICAL THAT BULL'D PICK ON THE WEAKEST PERSON in the room. Honestly, I don't know why that broccoli wasn't thrown at me. He should've thrown it at me. Not Kell. She doesn't even know him.

Listen to me. I'm rationalizing that I should be bullied. I am sick.

Everyone is putting away their trays and walking over to group. Brian wheels Dirt Face over, so I'm off the hook. Thank God. I really don't know if I could've controlled myself. He makes me sick.

Andrew is already in the group room, sitting in the

same seat as yesterday, but he's not alone. There's this huge muscle-bound orderly sitting behind him, against the wall. I'm guessing he's there to make sure Andrew keeps his anger under control.

But then the orderly gets up and tells Lisa he'll be standing right outside if she needs him. I guess he can't be *in* the room for group. Probably something to do with patient privacy and stuff.

"Oh, Jimmy, we'll be fine," Lisa says.

Lisa gets group going and we're off. While she's talking, I notice that Bull has positioned himself next to Kell in the circle. I swear, if he messes with her during group, I . . . I . . .

I won't do anything.

Kell's body language screams, *Get away from me!* She's sitting on one butt cheek, legs crossed away from him, arms crossed too, whole body facing the other direction, including her head. I see her journal is lying right under her chair. And he's just sitting there with a smug grin on his face, staring at her, like he wants to take a bite out of her.

Lacey starts today and goes into how much she hates her mother and her mother's boyfriend. Again. The whole story. Again. We all listen. Well, I'm not really listening. I keep stealing glances over at the Bull/Kell scene across the circle. She hasn't moved a muscle since group started. I wonder if her legs are cramping. Mine would. Bull hasn't broken his stare either. He's not even pretending to listen to Lacey's story. Again.

Lacey finishes talking. More tissues for her.

Nikole reaches over and squeezes her knee. She is so cool. Lacey gets up and hugs Nikole. More tears.

Lisa just lets this all happen.

Then they go back to their seats and sniffling is the only sound.

"So, William, Kell. What seems to be going on over there?" Lisa says. She is a bold woman.

Kell ignores her. Bull snaps out of his attack stare. "Nothing."

"Really? Nothing? I'm not so sure you're being honest, William. Kell? Would you like to share today?" Lisa pushes.

It's like Kell's wrapped in some invisible tape. She doesn't move. It doesn't even look like she's breathing.

"Okay, Kell, you don't want to share today. That's fine. But know this, we are all in pain in this room. Every patient here has gone through tremendously difficult times. Do you realize that? That we're all hurting?"

Kell doesn't move.

Lisa purses her lips and does a small nod. "William? Would you like to?"

"Nah, I'm good," he says.

Andrew comes alive and laughs. He says that if Bull were good, he wouldn't have a hole in his leg and a cast on his wrist *or* be sitting in this circle.

That doesn't make Bull smile.

Andrew says, "Come on, dude. We're all messed up, or we wouldn't be here. Like Lisa said. Right? I'm probably more effed than you, believe me. Anyone else here have a stepdad who has called him a moron since he was six? Called him retarded almost every day? In front of his brother—his real son? Said *he* was the reason his real dad left? That it was all his fault? Told him he wished someone else would just get rid of him, so he wouldn't have to see his face every day? Anyone? Yeah, we're all messed up in this room, William. None of us are good."

"Andrew, how did that make you feel?" Lisa asks. "These things your stepdad has said to you over the years."

Even I think I know the answer to this question.

"Like shit, that's how. Like a pile of—like a pile of nothing," he says. Then he goes quiet. Lisa tries to keep him talking.

"How does nothing feel?"

Wow, that's a good question, a really good question. How *does* nothing feel? This seems to have stumped Andrew as well, because he shrugs his shoulders and tells her he doesn't know. I try to answer the question in my head. How does nothing feel? How does nothing feel?

It feels like pain, pain every day. Your brain knows you are nothing and this causes pain. The pain grows in every cell of your body, like a disease that eats you from the inside out. Soon you're only a shell, because there is nothing left on the inside. No heart, no thinking, no emotions. Just a skin that walks around all day hurting.

That's how nothing feels.

I wish I had the guts to say this out loud. But I don't. I have no courage, so I sit and stare at Andrew. It looks like he's got something to say now.

"Nothing feels like nothing. I don't feel anything anymore."

"That's not true, Andrew. You feel anger," Lisa says. Lisa is right. We all saw Andrew's anger yesterday. We know he feels anger. So does the table he pounded on.

"Anger is something," Lisa says. She's really determined today.

I can't tell if this is making Andrew angry. He's got a wicked scowl on his face and his arms are crossed. I hope he doesn't start punching, because I'm only one seat away from him, and Nikole is next to him. I don't know what I'd do if he hurt Nikole. Even by accident. I look at Nikole and know that I would protect her; I would. For the first time in my life, I feel a little courage. I really would protect her.

Then I remember the big guy just outside the door, and I feel even more brave. He'd back me up. It's his job.

Brian breaks the silence. "Well, I'm leaving today right after group. I think I'm ready."

"Of course you're ready, Brian. It's because you *want* to live. For forever, remember?" Lacey says with a wink. "Don't be afraid."

Nikole says, "Well, guess what? I feel afraid, because *I'm* leaving tomorrow and I don't know how it's going to be when I go home."

My courage is sucked up by the vacuum of her words.

"Tomorrow?" I ask. Out loud. In front of the whole circle. Now all eyes are on me, except for Kell's, of course. She's still in her own dark world.

"Yeah, tomorrow. I was here for two days before you got here," she says directly to me. Then, to the group, "Doctor Billings saw me yesterday and said tomorrow's the day."

Lacey tells us she's leaving tomorrow too and swears she, Brian, and Nikole can make it out there. She says this with tears rolling down her cheeks.

"Thanks, Lace. You really think so?" Nikole asks. She seems like a little girl right now, not the fearless wonder I've seen the past two days.

"Yeah. We *can*. Besides, you and Brian are, like, the bravest

ones in this circle. Just keep your heads straight. Brian, live your life for you. You know?" Lacey turns to Nikole. "Your boyfriend's friends are going to need you when you get out of here. I don't know what they've been doing without you all these days, I swear."

*What happened to "I think we're going to be okay?"* I scream in my head. *What about our wishes? Our dreams? You can't leave me in here alone!*

Nikole smiles at her. "Those guys all call me Queenie because I'm the only girl in the group. Isn't that an awesome nickname?"

Lacey says, "You can do it, Queenie. I swear."

"So can you, Lacey," Nikole tells her.

"We all can," Brian says. "We just have to *want* to."

Lisa clears her throat. "Brian, Lacey, Nikole, you have made big strides in here. You should be proud of your clear thinking. And I second what Lacey said: You *can* do it. You *are* strong enough. Don't underestimate yourselves."

Nikole wipes her tears with the sleeves of her sweatshirt and smiles.

What about us here? We need her, too. She can't just leave. I need her.

# Bull

MAN, THIS GIRL IS CRAZY. SHE HASN'T MOVED IN, like, twenty minutes—not even to scratch her head or shake her foot or scribble crap in her precious notebook. Nothing. And she can wrap her one leg around the other one like a pretzel.

I have no idea what's been going on in the circle. I haven't taken my eyes off of this nut since I sat down, except when Lisa asked what was going on over here. The thought of whispering something in *her* ear comes to me, and I wish I wasn't in this freakin' wheelchair prison. I could never get close enough. If I could, I'd tell her she has pretty eyes.

No, I wouldn't. I'm too much of a chickenshit.

The girls are crying again. Great. Do I care why? No. But wait a second—did Victor's girlfriend and the "I swear" girl say they're leaving tomorrow? I turn my head a little bit so I can hear. I don't take my eyes off of Freaky, though. Yep, his girlfriend's outta here tomorrow. So's Lacey. And she's filling her head with "You can do anything" garbage. I think they're all gonna be the same messed-up group of psychos when they get out of here. Everyone's going back to the same messed-up places they came from. Even Brian. The same messed-up lives. They'll all probably be back here soon.

Except me.

I'm never going back to my apartment. Notice how I'm not calling it "home"? I don't have a home, and I never have. The shore is calling me. As soon as I get out of here, I'm going straight to the shore. I didn't try to kill myself. I'm more okay than all of them put together. I don't even belong here.

Did Victor just talk? Yeah, he did. He's probably going to start blubbering about his girlfriend leaving. I've seen him cry before, and his nose runs. Let me rephrase that: I've *made* him cry before. I wonder how Nikole will like looking at his snot. I really don't care about Victoria's boogers.

I go back to staring at the black-haired kook. She has a mole on her right ankle. No, wait, it's her left ankle. She's all tangled up. Her sweatshirt is way too big for her and is hanging off her shoulder. I can see her black bra strap. I picture how she looks when she's not wearing hospital-issued sweats and slippers.

I see black, all black. Black boots, black backpack, black makeup, all black. Does she have any friends out there? A boyfriend maybe? If she does, he probably has piercings and tattoos and combat boots. Damn, I want to know her story. I have a million questions. Where does she live? Go to school? What is her favorite thing to do? What the hell does she write in that book of hers? Anything in there about me? Does she have any brothers or sisters? Does she drive yet? Smoke? How did she try to kill herself? What made her do it? What is she afraid of? What would it be like to hug her? Make out with her? Touch her?

Great, I have a boner.

I have to stop looking at her. At least these sweats are big and loose, and I'm sitting down. No one can tell. God, at least I hope to shit they can't tell.

Group is over. Kell unravels herself and walks out. Everyone else gathers around Brian and does the whole good-bye thing. I like the dude and all but come on, I've only known him for, like, two days. And I don't know how to wish people well or any of that shit.

"I hope you lose weight," is what I say to Brian. That's about as emotional as I can get.

"Thanks. Me too," he says, and we shake hands. "But I'll always weigh less than an elephant. Right?"

I laugh. "Right."

Brian waves to everyone and then walks out.

Andrew offers to wheel me to the common room.

"Yeah, cool," I say.

"That chick is the craziest one out of all of us, dude," he tells me.

I play dumb, "Who?"

"Kell. The one you've been staring at for an hour. She's hot and everything, in a crazy kind of way, but she really *is* crazy. I overheard Agnes tell Ellie that this is her third time in here, and she's only sixteen. That's one effed-up girl."

"I was just messin' with her, you know, trying to make her crack," I say.

"Wrong girl to mess with. I swear to God I think she plots out ways to fuck people up in that book she writes in. I heard her talking with Lisa the day she got here, and Lisa asked her how she'd been since juvenile detention. The girl's been in jail. Lacey told me it was because she stabbed her stepdad. He didn't die, but she is cray-zee."

We're in the common room now, and I look around for

her. That story doesn't scare me. Kell's in her usual spot in the corner, facing the window, her back to the room, hand flying across the page. Her feet are up on the windowsill, and she's resting her back on the table. If I wasn't in this stupid wheelchair, I'd sneak up behind her and read what she's writing.

"I'd stay away from her, dude," Andrew says.

Like I'd listen to this guy. I don't even know him, and besides, he's not the most reliable person in here. He can shove his opinions up his butt.

Her slippers are off. She has really nice feet, and her toenails are painted . . . black.

# Victor

AFTER BRIAN LEAVES, WE ALL HEAD TO THE COMMON room, and I watch some TV show on penguins. Nikole tries three or four times to engage me in conversation, and I give her one word answers. I want her to think I'm really into this show. That I'm a penguin lover.

The penguins could be tap-dancing in soccer cleats and I'd have no idea. I'm not watching the show. I'm staring at the TV and falling apart, one cell at a time. My heart is ripping itself in two. As the credits roll I am officially a broken guy.

But I think I love her.

I close my eyes and pretend to sleep. Talking is not

an option for me. Nikole's voice rises above Lacey's and Andrew's. Even Bull's. And his voice used to be the one I'd listen for in the hallways at school. No one else exists in this common room.

Only Nikole.

I battle in my head. I'm wasting precious time with her by phony-napping. I should be talking with her, memorizing the tone of her voice. Committing her face to a secret place in my brain. But I'm unable to move.

Nikole laughs. The sound fills my head, and I do everything in my power to store it somewhere inside me. But my heart has no room. It lies inside my chest in two quivering mounds, torn clear in half. I can feel it. She laughs again. It's a rich, deep laugh, not like the girls at school, who laugh all twittery and giggly. Nikole laughs like she means it.

Everyone thinks I'm sleeping because they all ignore me. I sit there with my eyes closed for what feels like hours. Eventually I hear Agnes come in and announce dinner. "Best night of the week, everybody: pizza."

I "wake up" and stretch to make my nap authentic. Nikole stands in front of me. I do my best to show no sign of my inner turmoil and smile at her. She reaches up, tousles my hair, and says, "You were out like a light."

"Yeah," I say. Fake yawn.

Nikole smiles and links her arm in mine, and we walk to the cafeteria. Her arm, warm and real, sends life into me. My skin prickles, but the connection is broken when we take our seats. I remain torn.

I'm not hungry. I don't touch my dinner tray. I keep stealing glances at Nikole. Tomorrow? She's leaving tomorrow? That's ruined everything for me. I was so excited about getting to call my grandmother. Now I don't care about anything. Again.

Lacey is chirping away like a bird on speed, and I wish she'd shut up. I want Nikole to talk. I want to hear her voice again and concentrate on it. But she doesn't have a chance. Lacey is going on and on about how good Nikole will be out there on her own, and how she's her inspiration, she swears.

Tape? Does anyone have a piece of tape?

Nikole brilliantly makes her stop talking by asking me a question. "So, Victor, you're not hungry?"

I look down at my perfect platter and say, "No, I hate pizza." I can't believe I just said that. I love pizza. I could live on pizza. I'd eat it for breakfast, that's how much I love pizza. And I told her I hate pizza. Why am I so stupid? That's all I could come up with? That I hate pizza? Why can't I tell her that I don't want her to go? And that the thought of not seeing her big brown eyes and curly blond hair every day makes me numb inside? That it actually makes my stomach cramp? Why can't I tell her those things?

Because I don't know how, that's why. I don't know how to talk to people. I especially don't know how to talk to girls. But bottom line, I don't know how to talk to people. I don't think I've ever thought about this before. I think this is my biggest problem, besides having parents who don't know I exist. I don't know how to talk to people.

I'm not a good person.

People know how to talk to other people. It's part of being human.

Maybe I'm an alien.

I can't stay here. I have to leave, right now. I tell them I'm going to go back to my room, that I'm bored. They all look confused. No wonder—it was another stupid thing to say.

I start pacing in my room, thankful Bull isn't in here in his wheelchair, because I'd have a much smaller space to walk around. I walk back and forth between the window and the door, over and over again. On one of my walks past Bull's side I see a newspaper clipping on his nightstand. It stops me in my tracks. Bull Mastrick reads the newspaper? I find this shocking. I didn't know he even knew how to read.

I look toward the door. No one is coming, so I walk over and quickly pick up the clipping. It's a poem. This shocks me even more. Bull reads poetry? I immediately turn it over expecting to see a cartoon; that's about all I can picture Bull reading out of a newspaper. But there is just part of an advertisement for shoes. The clipping seems old, and I handle it more gently when I turn it back over.

I check the doorway again. Nothing. And I read the poem. When I get to the end, the last line about waiting for no one and filling *yourself* up, my hands starts to shake. My hands never shake. Well, that's not completely true; they only shake when I'm about to cry. It's this weird thing my body does. This time it's no different. My eyes fill up and let loose.

I cry because I am almost filled up. With Nikole.

And she's walking out the door tomorrow.

K. M. Walton

# Bull

VICTORIA DISAPPEARED FROM DINNER. I WAS TALKING with Andrew and I looked up at one point and his seat was empty. His tray was untouched. After ten minutes or so I asked Lacey to pass it down to me. If the dick was going to leave a tray full of perfectly good pizza, then hell, I'd eat it.

I watched Kell play with her gum all through dinner, watched her write, and watched her run her fingers through her greasy hair. I don't know why her dirty hair doesn't bother me. Usually that would be something I'd rag on someone for, but I don't want to make fun of her.

Later I try to get comfortable in bed, but I'm having

problems with it. My stitches are so itchy. Ellie told me it's because I'm healing. She said she'd come in here and tie my hands to the bed if I scratched them. The thought of her tying me to my bed makes me feel woozy. I have a good ten-minute fantasy on that one. But I promised her I wouldn't scratch, so I don't.

I look at the clock and it's 1:03 a.m. I'm wide awake. Doofus is snoring like a champ next to me, so I know he's out. Why can't I sleep? I forgot to ask Ellie for a book today. Shit, I would kill for a book.

A shadow walks by my closed curtain. Ellie never comes around on this side. A hand pulls back the drape.

It has chipped black nail polish.

What the . . . ?

Kell slinks inside my curtain and has her finger up to her mouth, shushing me. At least she's not *giving* me the finger this time. Before I can think about what is happening, Kell crawls over my bed and lays down next to me with her head on my shoulder.

What the . . . ?

She shushes me again and takes my left hand, the one with the cast on it, and puts it on her boob.

What the . . . ?

Her boob. My casted hand is on her boob. Insta-boner.

I pull my hand away. Why did I just pull my hand away? What the hell is the matter with me? She puts it back where it just was and whispers, "I know you want me."

Uh, duh.

"Why are you doing this?" I take my hand off, again. What a stupid thing to say. Why would I question her? She put my hand there twice. Twice!

"Because I'm horny, you idiot." She reaches for my hand again, *and I pull my hand back!* "Wait, are you gay?" she asks me. "Because if you're gay, I'm cool with that."

"No," I tell her, "I'm not gay."

"Then what's your problem?"

"I don't have a problem." Oh, I'm so convincing.

"If you're not gay, and you don't have a problem, then why won't you touch me?"

Good question. I go for the easy answer.

"I don't know."

"You're weird," she says.

"So are you."

This whole situation is weird. I have the girl I've been drooling over all day curled up on me, in my bed, putting *my* hand on *her* boob, and I just called her weird. Really romantic.

"I know you didn't try to kill yourself," she says.

Wait, hold up. How would she know that? How *could* she know that?

I huff. "You don't know anything about me," I say. God she smells so good.

"I know you smell like springtime," she says, "right after it rains."

That must be the hospital soap. No one has ever told me I smelled like anything except for my pop. He would sometimes tell me my breath smelled like dog crap in the morning. I wish I'd brushed my teeth before bed. What if my breath smells like dog crap?

"Don't you want to know how I know your secret?" she asks.

I don't know how to answer her. If I say yes, that'll mean I do have a secret. If I say no, she might leave my bed. I tell her I don't have a secret.

Then she kisses me.

It is a perfect, vanilla-filled kiss. No tongue, just lips touching in all the right places. I have no idea what I'm doing, but it's clear she does. She is the first girl I've ever kissed. Yeah, I know, I'm sixteen. Whatever.

She pulls back, then gives me a peck.

I love her.

Her hair smells like flowers, and I try to breathe her in

K. M. Walton

without being creepy. She washed her hair for me. She's got her head on my chest again, and I would give anything to have the balls to reach over and stroke her head. But my casted wuss of an arm stays by my side.

"I really don't know your secret. I was just trying to fake you out," she says. She lifts her head and kisses me again. It's a real good thing I'm already lying down, because I swear to God I might pass out with her deliciousness. This time she licks my lips with her tongue, and my crotch is about to burst. I'm thinking that she's not a virgin. I am fine with this, as long as she keeps kissing me like she's kissing me right now. She does. We make out for like a half hour, maybe more, who knows.

"The nurses come in here every hour, you know," I say in between kisses. Again, the dumbest thing to say, ever. Why don't I just push her out of my bed and hit the call button?

She puts her head on my chest. "I know. They don't scare me."

My mind goes back to all the questions I wanted to ask her. I decide to go big.

"What *are* you afraid of?" I can't believe I asked her.

She lifts her head and looks me right in the eye. "Nothing," she says. Then she lays her head back down on my chest.

"Oh, come on, everyone's afraid of something," I tell her,

even though if anyone asked me the same question, I'd have an identical answer.

"What are *you* afraid of?" she asks.

Crap. Now what?

I can't say, "nothing" because that would be stupid, and I do not want her to think I'm stupid. Stupid guys don't get kissed by hot girls. I could tell her about my pop and how he beats the shit out of me, but I'm not scared of that anymore, just sort of numb to it. I could tell her about being afraid I'll never find my real dad, and how he probably won't want anything to do with me. But I can't do that. It's too complicated.

"Losing my bike. I'm afraid of losing my bike," I say. There: easy, truthful, not too mushy.

"What are you, eleven? Don't you have a car?" she asks.

I blew it. No more kisses for me.

"No, I'm not eleven, and no, I don't have a car. It's a BMX bike, not a tricycle. My bike was almost four hundred bucks," I say, slightly annoyed. I don't want to be too annoyed, because I don't want her to leave my bed. Ever.

"Your turn." I'm not letting her off the hook.

"I already told you. Nothing. I'm not afraid of anything. Or anyone."

"That's stupid."

Did I really just say that? Did I really just call her stupid?

Am I for real? I don't deserve any more kisses because *I'm* stupid, not her.

She sits up and runs her fingers through her hair over and over again. Her back is to me. My side is instantly not as warm as it was when she was snuggled next to me. I don't like how this feels.

She turns around and her face is twisted in anger. "You don't know anything about me, asshole."

"Exactly. I don't. Why do you think I asked you that question?" I desperately want her to lie back down. To kiss me again.

"Yeah, well, if you knew anything about me, you wouldn't be kissing me or sniffing my hair. You don't know anything."

Man, I thought she couldn't tell that I was smelling her hair.

"You wouldn't even talk to me, let alone make out with me. I'm the crazy girl, the one everyone loves to mock and whisper about. Everyone loves a good crazy girl. And I'm her."

"I know one thing. Everyone wants to be loved without conditions or restrictions, limitations or boundaries." Whoa. I pulled out the big guns.

This takes her by surprise. The big lug in the wheelchair is deeper than she expected. He just said something interesting.

I can tell by the look on her face that I've confused her. She looks like she's smelling a pile of horse manure.

"What? What are you talking about?" she stammers.

I go for the repeat. Basically because I can't come up with anything else to say.

"I said, '*Everyone* wants to be loved without conditions or restrictions, limitations or boundaries.'"

"Did you make that up? No, there's no way you made that up. But where did you hear that? Did you *read* that some-where, like on a card or something?"

I think she's just insulted me, but I don't care because she's curled up next to me again. She could say anything to me right now, and I wouldn't care.

"No. Well, sort of, but—what do you write in that book?" I blurt out.

"What do you care?"

I don't really know why I care, but I do. I've been dying to snatch it from her hands and read the whole thing. "I don't know. I guess I'm curious."

"Yeah, well, wouldn't you like to know," she says with a grin. Then she leans down and kisses me again. Full force kiss. Tongue and all.

Nurse/linebacker Agnes throws the curtain back and booms, "Party's over, Kell. Out!"

I get the scowl from Agnes too. Kell leans down, gives me a peck, and whispers in my ear, "You sure know how to kiss, gimpy." Stunned, I watch her hop out of my bed. She turns and blows me a kiss, then skips out of the room.

She is the wackiest girl I've ever met. And she left her journal/notebook/diary thing on my nightstand.

# Victor

I DON'T WANT TO GET OUT OF BED. IF I GET OUT OF bed, that means the day has started, and I don't want this day to start. Bull has already showered. I had to wheel him in there an hour ago, and then wheel him back when he was done. I crawled back into bed after both times and pretended it was yesterday.

"What, are you crying over there because you're girl-friend's leaving today? Hurry up and get ready, I'm starving!" he shouts through the curtain. Oh, how I wish the curtain was made of soundproof steel so I would not have to hear another human being's voice. Especially his.

I squeeze my hands into fists under my blankets as rage bursts from my brain like a bullet. The covers are off. I'm out of bed. I'm standing right in front of him. I pull back one of my fists and punch him in his face. I know it landed, because

1. I think I broke my knuckle, and
2. His lip is bleeding.

I have completely lost my mind.

I just punched Bull Mastrick in the face. Me, Victor Konig, punched Bull Mastrick in the face. Me. I did this. It appears that he is in just as much shock as I am, because he doesn't say anything. He doesn't even do the instinctual hand-to-face maneuver you always see in the movies after someone gets punched in the mouth. He sits there like a statue. A bleeding statue.

"Don't you ever talk about her again," I spit out at him. Then I turn around and head straight for the bathroom to assess the damage to my hand. It's not broken, but it hurts a ton. I look at myself in the mirror to see if I look any different after punching someone. I smile. You have no idea how happy I am that Bull Mastrick was the first person I've ever punched. Immediately I wish the bathroom door had a lock on it. Even though he's in a wheelchair, I can picture him pushing his way in here and leveling me.

I hear Ellie come in our room.

"Oooooh, what happened to you?" she asks Bull.

Through the door I hear him answer, "Smacked my face on that table trying to reach for my water."

He lied. Why did he lie? I know it wasn't to protect me. But why did he lie? Pride. Bull lied because he doesn't want anyone to know I nailed him. Victoria, Dicktoria, whatever, punched him and made him bleed.

"Let me get you some ice, William. Hold on," she says.

"Nah, I'm good."

She says she's going to get him a wet washcloth.

"Victor's in there," he says.

"Not a problem. I'll be right back."

I'm not coming out of here until he's gone. I'm glad I'm in a bathroom because I just might crap myself. Punching Bull in the face is the most fearless thing I've ever done. And now I'm scared shitless. He will kill me. I know this for sure.

I hear grunting. He's wheeling himself over here to dismember me. I think he kicks the door. He growls, "You tell anyone about what you just did and I'll—"

"How did you get all the way over here, William?" Ellie chirps. Thank God she's back. I have no desire to hear what he'd do to me if I told anyone what I just did. "Here, put this on your lip. I filled it with ice."

K. M. Walton

"Thanks," he says.

There's a light knock on the door. "Victor?"

"Yes?"

"I'll wheel William over to breakfast, okay?"

"Yeah, fine," I tell her.

I take the hottest shower of my life. My skin is red, and I'm sweating . . . in the shower. I'm trying to wash the fear away. But it's crazy-glued all over me.

All over me.

# Bull

I CAN'T BELIEVE THAT PRICK PUNCHED ME.

Then I think, I can't believe it took so long for that prick to punch me. I know I deserve it. I know I deserve to have the crap beaten out of me. I get that. I just can't believe he really hit me. He must really like Nikole. Love does weird things to guys. I should know. I stayed up all night reading Kell's journal cover to cover. But it's not a journal at all, it's a novel. I guess I don't need to ask Ellie for anything to read now.

Believe it or not, Kell's writing a book. It's about a little boy who has no parents and lives on the streets, and finds out he has magic powers after he spends the night with a talking rat. I couldn't put it down. But I kept stopping and resting the book on my chest and thinking how freaking cool this girl is. I mean, she's writing a book. A real book.

I also had some trouble getting Kell and her boob out of my head. And her lips. And her flowery-smelling hair. And how warm she felt next to me. And her vanilla breath. And her long eyelashes. And her chipped nail polish. And her tongue.

Like I said, weird things.

I'm in the cafeteria now, and she isn't here yet. I've looked over at the big table, oh, like, five million times already. I keep checking the door too, but she hasn't come in. I can't wait to tell her what a good writer she is.

Victor hasn't come either, the wimp. He's probably still hiding in the bathroom. I wonder if he'll show for group, which, according to Lisa, starts in five minutes. Kell walks in. She makes her sweatsuit look so hot. My eyes follow her. She walks right up to me, and I smile.

"Where is it, asshole?" No smile.

I don't get it. She had *her* tongue in *my* mouth last night; she put *my* hand on *her* chest last night. I don't get it.

"Good morning to you, sunshine," I say, and hold up her notebook.

She grabs it and walks away.

She didn't even give me a chance to compliment her or

tell her my favorite parts, like when the kid figures out he can shoot laser beams from his eyes and he zaps the bad guy right in the nuts. I literally felt a sting in my crotch as I read that part, it was that good.

Andrew says to me, "Look, there goes the Queen of Crazy."

If I wasn't in the wheelchair I'd have probably knocked him out, so I throw an insult his way instead. One that will sting. "She isn't any crazier than you, retard." I grind in the retard part because I know that's what his stepdad called him. I'm not proud of saying it, but I have to make it hurt. And it does. He's up out of his chair like a pouncing cat, about to split open my lip on the other side, when muscle guard Jimmy jumps up and gets in between us. We all know how big Jimmy is, and I'm really thankful, because he is about the only thing in the room that would've blocked Andrew's insane rage from landing on my face.

Nurses and orderlies fly in, and Andrew's removed like a criminal, hands behind his back. I feel bad again. He screams that I'm an asshole the whole way down the hall. I guess it really was kind of low, but he called the girl I love crazy. Yeah, I said it, I love her. I want to protect her, which is definitely a new feeling for me. I've never felt that way about another person before. The only thing I've ever wanted to protect is my bike. She's way better than a bike. My bike doesn't have soft lips or smell like vanilla. She's just way better.

K. M. Walton

I tell my side of the story to Agnes, and, well, let's just say she thinks I'm the victim here. She tells me I'm lucky the guard got in between us, and I laugh and tell her I've been in fights with dudes way bigger than Andrew. She pats me on the head kind of hard and tells me to be good, like I'm a dog.

I know I did the right thing, and for the first time in my life an adult agrees with me. I'm not sure, but I think what I'm feeling is pride. It's foreign to me, though, so I'm not 100 percent sure. And that kind of sucks.

Lacey is flipping out at Andrew attacking me, and she's panting and telling me I shouldn't have called him that. My pride speaks up and I clarify things for her. "Duh, I know that," I tell her, "but I didn't have a choice."

"It was just so mean. I swear. So, so mean. God, what are you, like, in love with Kell or something?" she says while blinking like a looney tune.

Uh-oh, I'm getting mad again. I keep my cool though; I do not want to be the next one escorted out of here with my hands behind my back, broken wrist and all. Ouch.

"I don't care about her," I lie.

"Then why did you get Andrew all hyped up?"

I shift in my wheelchair, trying my best to not lose it on her. "I don't know. Because I wanted to."

"Well, it wasn't cool. I swear. You shouldn't have done that.

He's already gotten in trouble for his other freak-out. Now they'll put him back in solitary because he's a 'danger' to us." She says the word danger with her fingers doing air quotes.

I reply with my own air quotes and say, "I. Don't. Care." Air quote. Which is a big lie. I do care. And I actually feel pretty bad about it. Just then Kell gets up from her table and walks toward me. Everything else in the room disappears; it's all just her. I stare at her and smile. She gives me the double finger again.

What the . . . ?

K. M. Walton

# Victor

I TRIED TO STAY IN THE BATHROOM, BUT ELLIE CAME and knocked and started asking a ton of questions. I told her I didn't feel good, like I was going to throw up. She brought me some ginger ale and crackers and had me lay down. No temperature, tonsils looked good, eyes clear, strong heartbeat— she told me I just needed something in my stomach.

Ellie leaves me alone to rest, but I pace the length of my room a hundred times. Today is Nikole's last day. And I'm hiding out in my room. I gag a few times. The ginger-ale-mixed-with-vomit taste lingers in my mouth, each swallow a bitter reminder of what a weak, selfish jerk I am.

I actually tried my best to get out of group. That's how terrified I am of Bull's revenge. Ellie said missing group wasn't an option, unless I was unconscious. I seriously tried to think of ways to knock myself out, but I couldn't come up with anything.

So here I am, in group. I'm the first one here, except Lisa, of course. And some new guy with really bad acne. He looks pretty miserable. Lisa introduces him as Grant. He only nods, no smile. Believe me, I understand the discomfort he feels right now. She asks me who I'll be calling, since it's my fourth day and all. I tell her I'm calling my grandma, my nana.

"Not your parents?" she asks.

"They're in Europe right now. I don't even know where they are, actually." This makes my stomach lurch, and if I were near a toilet, I'd probably vomit.

"I see. How do you feel about this? About them not coming home?" she asks.

Even though Lisa's face is gentle and kind, I want to say, "How do you think I feel? It makes me feel like crap. It makes me feel unloved, unwanted, un-everything." But I'd never talk that way to an adult. So instead I say, "I don't know."

She says in a calm voice, "You don't know. Who do you think would know, then? You know, how *you* feel?"

Why do some people have to be so annoying?

"I don't know," is all I say. She probably thinks I'm as dumb as the chair I'm sitting on. Probably dumber. I look over at Grant to see if he has any reaction to our conversation.

"Well, Victor, you think about my question. Okay? It's okay to feel things, even if you're a guy. When a guy knows how he feels and why he feels that way, well, then he owns his feelings, which is healthy thinking. And healthy-thinking guys make great boyfriends, and friends, and sons, and even husbands."

The word boyfriend makes me think of Nikole again and how selfish I am. I should've been at breakfast with her. It was her last meal here, and I was hiding out in my room like a scared puppy. Lisa is right: I have really unhealthy thinking. My thinking is diseased and coughing and oozing green snot.

My mother hates the words "snot" and "boogie" and "booger." She basically hates anything inside the nose, no matter the color or consistency. If it's from the nose, she hates it. When I was little and sick, she made my father wipe my nose. When I was almost five, she said I had to be responsible for wiping my own nose from then on.

Why am I thinking about my mother?

Lisa is tapping my knee. She must think I'm really out of it—I'm having a full-blown conversation in my head, completely ignoring her. Talk about unhealthy thinking.

"Nikole's calling you," she says, and points to the doorway.

I look up and there she is. The first thing I notice is that she doesn't have her sweats on. She dressed in jeans and a really tight T-shirt with a cool, swirly design on the front. She looks pretty. She is waving me over, so I jump up.

"Hey," I say.

"Hey," she says. She grabs my hand and pulls me out into the hall.

"So, I'm leaving. I wanted to say good-bye to you."

I don't know what to say. You know how in books people always say the room started spinning at the dramatic part? Well, it's true: the hallway started spinning.

"You all right? You look really pale," she says.

I start breathing like a dog in the sun. If I don't sit down, I'm going to fall down. I plop into a cross-legged heap on the floor and rest my chin on my chest. I breathe in . . . she's leaving. I breathe out . . . right now. I breathe in . . . she's leaving. I breathe out . . . right now.

"Victor? Are you okay?" she repeats.

I lift my head. "I'm sick. I almost didn't come to group. I threw up this morning." All lies.

She rubs my back and asks if she should go get a nurse. I tell her no, I'll be fine. Another lie.

"Well, I wanted to see you before I left. I'm . . . I'm . . . wow, this is harder than I thought it was going to be."

I say, "Tell me about it."

"I wrote down my cell number and my e-mail, and I'll friend you on Facebook, okay?"

"I'm not on Facebook. My parents are insane about the computer," I tell her.

I drop my head again. It feels heavy on my neck. Reality is heavy. She has friends that call her Queenie, had a boyfriend, is a cheerleader—she has a life, a life that is far, far away from mine. She's beautiful and funny and laughs with gusto. Me, I'm a nobody with no one and nothing. A total dork.

She puts a piece of paper in my hand and closes my fingers around it. Her hand stays on top of mine, and it feels beyond perfect.

"Look, you got me through this place, Victor. You are a good person, and I want you to be happy. I will miss you every single day for the rest of my life, I swear." Her Lacey imitation makes me smile, and I raise my head to look at her.

"*You* got me through this place too. *You* are a better person than I'll ever be. And I will miss you even after I'm dead, I swear," I say.

Her beautiful eyes are filled with tears, and she lifts my hand up and kisses my palm. Then she puts my open hand on her face and holds it there against her soft, warm cheek. I want to kiss her so bad it hurts.

She leans in and does it for me. It's a soft kiss, right on the mouth. I imagine this is what doing drugs feels like. I'm cloudy with it, all fogged up with goodness, and happy. She whispers in my ear, "Just be happy. Stay alive, Victor. You're worth it."

It must be the pure happiness from my first kiss that makes me do this, but I grab both of her cheeks and pull her in for another kiss. This time, *I* kiss *her*. She had been squatting down, so my kiss makes her fall forward onto her knees, and she is totally kissing me back.

The rest of the kids come out of the cafeteria right in the middle of our kiss and start making smooching noises and somebody whistles. Nikole pulls away and whispers in my ear again, "Stay alive. You're worth it." Then she hops up and starts her good-byes with everyone else. Lacey joins in, and there's a lot of hugging and high-fiving. Nikole and Lacey link arms and declare that they're outta here.

I watch her curls bounce as she talks. Her kiss lingers on my mouth and I lick my lips. I had my first kiss in the hallway of a psych ward with a girl who tried to kill herself a few days ago.

And I can't stop smiling about it.

# Bull

WOULD YOU LOOK AT DORK OF THE UNIVERSE? Making out in the hallway with the hot blonde. They're putting on quite a show for Jimmy the guard. I would've bet my bike that would never happen in my lifetime. This place is nuts, completely nuts. Today is the fourth day, and I think I'm crazier than when I got here. Everybody really is crazy here.

Especially Kell.

What the hell is with her giving me the fingers again? What is that all about? One minute she's all over me and the next I'm ignored and dissed. Andrew was right: she is the Queen of Crazy. Now I feel even more guilty for making him go berserk again. I'm staying away from her. She'll probably kill me in my sleep. Leave it to me to fall in love with a maniac.

Lisa eventually gets us all in our seats, which is pretty hard to do after Nikole and Lacey's good-byes. Victor seems pretty bummed. He's delusional if he thinks a girl like that would go for him out in the real world. He wears a golf shirt and tan pants to school every day. She's totally hot with a great laugh. Get real.

And there's some zit-faced new guy in the circle. Ha. He looks about as happy as I was my first day.

Lisa starts group with, "Everyone, this is Grant. Grant, this is everyone."

Grant doesn't even look up.

Andrew's out of solitary, and he looks high. He must be on some good meds, because he actually grins at me.

Lisa smiles. "Now I'd like to discuss how you feel about Brian, Nikole, and Lacey leaving."

Not me. Don't care.

No one says a word.

Then she turns to Victor. "Victor, you got pretty close with Nikole, and you haven't shared in group yet. How about you tell us why Nikole is nice?"

Victor looks like he just farted out a watermelon.

"She just is, that's all," he says. I can't believe he said anything. He's such a wuss. Lisa isn't done with him, though.

"And why is that?" she asks gently. Man, am I glad she isn't interrogating me in front of the group, gentle voice or not. It could get ugly. I'm not sharing shit with these nutjobs.

He shrugs his shoulders as his answer. From where I'm sitting it looks like his hands are having a seizure. Maybe he's having a nervous breakdown or something. He has had a pretty crappy morning so far.

Lisa just stares at him and waits. Wow. Harsh.

He puts his hands underneath his legs and looks like he's in pain, like someone is trying to rip his head off or something. Lisa leans forward a bit in her chair. Apparently she cares what's going to come out of Victor's mouth. Me? Don't care at all.

"You can do this, Victor. It's okay to let it out, that's what we're all here for. That's what group is for," Lisa says.

Andrew chimes in with a groggy, "He doesn't want to, Lisa. Leave him alone."

Lisa purses her lips and then says gently, "Andrew, I acknowledge the fact that you're looking out for Victor. I appreciate it. But getting it out is the first step to healing. You know this." Lisa folds her hands on her lap. "Let me do my job, Andrew."

Andrew rolls his eyes. "Yeah. Sure. Whatever."

I had no idea Victor was this stubborn. I thought *I* was stubborn. He looks like if someone poked him with a pin, he'd explode all over the room. "Uncomfortable"—that's the perfect word to describe him. I don't blame him. Like I said, I'm not saying anything either. For once, I realize we have something in common. I'll say it again: This place does weird things to people.

Then he blows my "we have something in common" thought by saying, "She made me feel alive."

Okay, not bad. Short and to the point—not bad.

"What do you mean by 'alive'?" Lisa asks.

He scrunches up his face, and I can hear him breathing all the way across the room.

"Victor?" Lisa is one determined lady.

He keeps his head down and tells his story to the floor. "My parents never wanted me to be born. I was an accident; they tell me that every year on my birthday. They didn't take me on our trip to Europe because I didn't get perfect SAT scores. My perfect math score wasn't good enough. They didn't even wake me up and say good-bye. They left me a note on the counter, like I was the gardener. My dog died that day too. And she was the only thing that ever loved me. So I took my mom's sleeping pills. But my nana found me, and that's how I ended up here. Where I met Nikole. Nikole was the first human being to notice me. And she cared about what I thought. She looked me in the eye and laughed at things I said. She was the first girl I ever kissed. That's what I mean by alive."

Whoa.

He's not done. He raises his head and looks directly at me.

His voice is thick with volume and anger. "And you. You sit over there like you're the king of the jungle! Well, guess what, hard-ass? You're as fucked up as I am!"

I have nothing to say back to him. But it doesn't matter; he's yelling to the whole group now. About me.

"This asshole has bullied me since we were kids. Tortured me. Embarrassed me. Humiliated me. Beat the crap out of me. So many times, I can't count them all!" he yells, then he looks right back at me again. "You made me feel worthless." He's choking now, coughing out his words. "Worthless and stupid. Do you have any idea how much I hate you? How many times I wished you would just DIE?!"

Yeah, got nothing to say to that. Nothing at all.

"Remember when you punched me in the back? Punched the chocolate milk right out of me? You let me choke on it, and I almost died. Remember that? That was the day before I took the pills. You sealed the deal, Bull."

Is he blaming me? Yep, I think he's blaming me.

"Don't make me responsible for your crap life. You've got shitty parents," is the first thing out of my mouth. I really am an asshole. He's crying like a baby, spilling his guts to the whole room, and I don't have one nice thing to say? Not one?

He says, "Don't talk to me about shitty parents. Get beat up at home much? I've seen your bruises. I'm not stupid. I'm really good at listening; it's pretty easy when no one speaks to you for days on end. I heard kids talking about you and your grandfather all the way back when we were in seventh grade. Do you miss his fists? Did my punch this morning make you feel all nostalgic for home? You can go to hell, Bull."

Grant suddenly comes alive and is on his feet. He stops my pathetic one-armed attempt to wheel across the circle and pummel Victor. He pushes me right back into my spot in the circle and tells me to relax.

"Get off me, zit boy." Why do I always do that? Why do I always go for someone's weakness? I see Kell watching this whole scene, and I am embarrassed as hell. I've got to get away from these people, this place.

"I assume Bull is your nickname, William. Would you like to respond to Victor?" Lisa asks.

Hell yeah.

# Victor

NIKOLE'S KISS MUST'VE RELEASED SOME SORT OF courage or bravery juice that'd been locked in my brain, because it's flowing through my veins like crazy. I cannot believe I just said all that in front of these people, and Nikole wasn't even next to me, cheering me on. I did it on my own. I feel lighter. I'm serious, I really do. I actually feel lighter, and my hands have stopped shaking. I just wish Lisa didn't give him a chance to respond, because I don't want to hear anything he has to say. I just want group to be over so I can call my grandmother.

Here he goes. "Yeah, Bull's my nickname. And this dick

doesn't know anything about my life or my pop." Then he screams at me, "You don't know anything about me!"

Lisa calmly says, "Well, William, why don't you tell us about you? Like I told Victor, that's what group is for."

"I'm great. I love my life. There, I'm done," he says.

"Ha!" Kell says from across the room. The dark horse has spoken. This really takes Bull by surprise, and he looks shaken and nervous. Oh, what a glorious sight. Bull squirming like a slug in the sun.

"Kell, do you have something you'd like to say?" Lisa asks.

She shakes her head no and goes back to looking angry. She's clutching her notebook to her chest.

Apparently her lack of response ticks Bull off.

"What's the matter with you?!" he yells across the circle at her. This is, hands down, the most explosive group we've had. It makes Andrew's raging meltdowns seem like a tiny speck of nothing.

Kell puts her notebook on her lap, sticks her arms straight out toward Bull, and then slowly raises both of her middle fingers. Huh, interesting.

"Whatever," Bull says. He reaches up and rubs his baldish head with his good hand, then blows air through his nose. And he rolls his eyes.

Apparently this ticks Kell off.

"Whatever? That's your comeback?" she mocks. Then she whispers, "I thought you were different."

"You are the one who ignored me this morning and flipped me off in the caf. That was all you," Bull retorts.

She tells him she was trying to protect him. Then she calls him an idiot.

"Protect me from what? I don't get it."

"From me. I was trying to protect you from *me*," she cries out.

Lisa has a very pleased look on her face right now, like she's happy all of her loverlies are dumping their feelings on the floor today. Then it gets quiet, and Lisa lets it stay quiet. Everyone seems to have a real interest in the blue carpeting, because no one is looking anywhere else, except me. I'm stealing looks around the circle.

Bull stares at the floor and clears his throat. We all turn to him, expecting him to say something. But he doesn't. Lisa does.

"Kell, why would William need to be protected from you?"

"Because I *am* crazy. I know my diagnosis. I've read all about it online. Borderline personalities are nuts. And I'm nuts. He's too nice of a guy to get mixed up with me and my life."

The "Ha!" escapes my mouth involuntarily. Lisa looks at

me with raised eyebrows. I drop my eyes. I don't want to get into it again with Bull, but him being called a nice guy was just too much.

"Well, what if *you* don't get to make that decision?" Bull barks across the circle. Grant jumps. Apparently Grant is alive. "No matter how *borderline* you are?"

"It's *my* life, and I make my own decisions. And my life fucking rots. It always has!" she shouts.

"Join the club, Kell," Bull says.

Yeah, join the club.

"Guess what? I thought *you* were different," Bull says.

Uh, she *is* different.

"Oh, I'm cray-zee different, William, *cray-zee* different," she says wildly, with her hands shaking out in front her like she's doing a dance routine.

"I like you. And I like you just the way you are." I watch Bull swallow hard. I think he just blew his own mind.

Whoa. That took balls.

"I like *you*, just the way *you* are," she says.

Again, whoa. That took balls too.

Bull says, "And you are a really good writer. Like what's in that notebook should be a real book."

She stares at him and he stares back. Kell uncrosses her arms and sits on her hands. Bull does another head rub.

Kell looks back at Bull. "I left it in your room on purpose."

"I know," he says. "It was the best book I ever read. Better than anything, Kell. You're better than anything."

Now I feel like I'm eavesdropping on their private conversation. I seriously wonder if they remember they're sitting in a therapy circle with other people. I look at Grant, and he's back to looking comatose. So's Andrew—he might actually be sleeping.

And Lisa—she looks dreamy, sort of like she's taken a happy pill or something. It looks like I am the only one who wants the love train to crash, so I can move on and get out of here. I'd like to call my nana. God, isn't group over already anyway? It feels like we've been going and going and going. I look at my watch; we've gone over our hour. I feel compelled to announce this.

"Uh, Lisa, we're ten minutes over."

"Well, we certainly are. Did we get the party started today or what?" she asks.

I'm already out the door when I remember that I'm supposed to be pushing Bull around. I do an about-face. Jimmy the guard is shaking Andrew awake, and Kell is kneeling down next to Bull. Based on the way he's smiling, I'm thinking he'll be in a decent mood and might forget about retaliating for my punch. And it looks like I'm off the hook. Kell can wheel him around now. Hallelujah.

# Bull

I LIKE HEARING HER SAY MY NAME—MY REAL NAME.
She likes me. She said so in front of everyone. I can't believe
*I* said I liked *her* in front of everyone. But you know what? It
felt good to say it. It made it real.

Kell wheels me to the nurses' station. I want to see if my
mom called. She's allowed to call today, and she's probably
freaking out that I haven't been home to give her money. She
wasn't around when the gun went off and everything, so she'll
want to hear the whole messy story. Kell stops my wheelchair
and starts rubbing my head. I can hear Agnes and Ellie behind
the counter, shuffling papers, clicking on their keyboards.

Kell bends down and whispers in my ear, "You should let your hair grow out. You'd look so hot with longer hair."

I'm thinking she has no idea that her touching me, anywhere, produces blood flow to my lap. My arms go from resting on the armrests to covering up my growing crotch. I don't need her or Ellie seeing me like that. It's freakin' embarrassing.

Ellie appears from behind the counter. "William, Kell, how may I help you today?"

I'm sandwiched between the two hottest females, with a boner—isn't that great? I've got to clear my head. Clear. Head. Out.

"Has my mom called?" I ask.

"Let me check." She goes behind the counter, and I hear more rustling papers. "I don't see any messages for you, William."

I take a wild chance. "My pop call?"

"Nope, doesn't look like it."

I don't know why I thought either one of them would call. I feel stupid that I had Kell wheel me down here. I can't believe I thought they would've called. My face feels red, and I'm embarrassed. I bob my head quickly in an attempt to nod. Like I knew they wouldn't call. Ellie must realize I'm uncomfortable, because she smiles and tells me that I have a visitor who's been waiting in my room for five minutes.

A visitor? In *my* room? I didn't even know we were allowed to *have* visitors in here.

I take a wild chance, again. "My pop?"

"No, not your grandfather. It's your friend, Frank."

The old guy from the cemetery. Who leaves me bags of food with notes.

And a poem.

K. M. Walton

# Victor

"NANA? HI, IT'S VICTOR," I SAY INTO THE PHONE AT the nurses' desk. They actually have a private desk in the corner just behind their counter. It's not in a room or anything, but it faces the wall, so it's almost private.

"Oh, Victor. I've been a ball of worry waiting to hear your voice."

My nana is always a ball of worry. "I'm okay, Nana."

Wait, am I okay? I think I am. This is a big shock to me—like, colossal. I think I really am okay. I feel different.

"Are they feeding you well in there? Do you have clean clothes? Are you sleeping all right?"

"Nana, really, I'm okay. We eat pretty well, and we all have to wear sweatsuits, and they're clean, I promise."

"Ohhhh, Victor," she says softly, "when I found you. . . ." She's quietly crying into the phone. This makes me really upset. I'm not a big fan of people crying, but it really stinks when your nana is crying over something you did.

"Nana, I'm sorry. I *am* sorry. I wasn't thinking straight then. I'm sorry I didn't think of how you would feel. I . . . I . . ." I exhale into the phone. "I was in a lot of pain, Nana. And Jazzer died. And Mom and Dad left me behind because they are selfish people."

She huffs into my ear. I guess she is really mad at me. I don't know what else to say to her. I wish I could tell her how appreciative I am that she saved me. And how her voice in my head sounds more like home to me than any sound I've heard in my life.

"Your *parents*! Ha! I know your mother is my daughter, but she has done you wrong, Victor. I've never had the courage or the opportunity to tell you how I feel about how you've been raised. It all makes me so upset." My grandmother is fired up, all the whimpering gone from her voice. She is speaking with a fierceness I've never heard before. "I can't tell you how many times I've been a ball of worry over you up here, so far away from me, never getting to see you. . . ."

This makes me feel relief. And pride. I stare at the wall and let it sink in. The ward carries on behind me—people talk, other phones ring—but in this corner, I am beaming.

She has more to say. "I'll tell you what I've done, Victor. I've done quite a bit since your—oh, I hate to even say it—since your *suicide* attempt. What you've been through, the pain you must've been in. It's just so . . . well, you've got me now, sweetheart. I'm having my things sent up here. I'm taking the spare bedroom across the hall from you. I'm moving in. Oh, yes I am. I called your mother and told her you need me. I told her she should be ashamed of herself for not coming home to be with her boy. I told her you were a good boy, and she should be ashamed for not noticing what a good boy you are. That's what I told her. Oh, she tried arguing with me, even hung up on me once, but I just called her right back. Got your father on the phone then, gave him the business too. Yes I did. So you listen here, Victor. I will be here when you get home. I *will* be here."

I'm crying. I'm crying because she fought for me. She stood up for me.

My nana said she'll be there. For *me*.

# Bull

FRANK IS SITTING IN THE CHAIR OVER BY THE WINDOW, and he gets up when we come in. Kell kisses my cheek and whispers in my ear, "I'll miss you." Then she leaves us alone.

It takes me a second to clear my head from Kell, her kiss, and her private message.

"So, you've been eating my snacks, have you?" He grins.

"Yes, sir," I say. I've never called anyone "sir" in my entire life. Seriously. But he looks like he deserves to be called sir— like he could be on the poster for "Grandfather of the Year." Today he's got his gray hair combed and is wearing a button-up brown V-neck sweater.

We stare at each other. I have no idea what to say to the guy. I *want* to ask him why he's here and why he keeps leaving me food and why he put that damn poem in the bag. But I'm nervous and I don't want to sound like a dumbass. Luckily, he starts talking.

"I'm sure you're wondering why I've taken up such an interest in you, especially since we've never actually met," he says with a smile.

Whoa, he's a mind reader. Wild. I nod.

He keeps going. "I've noticed you at the graveyard for a long time. Never wanted to disrupt you there, though. I could see that the time you spent there was special to you. I could tell you needed that time."

Frank's good, because he never looked like he noticed me there, ever. He always looked like he was oblivious.

"Yes, sir." Is that all I can say to this guy? He's going to think I'm slow or something. In an effort to say anything, I blurt out, "How'd you get those brown bags in here?" Not, *Nice to meet you, thanks for visiting me.* I go right for the inquisition. Smooth.

"I knew you'd wonder about that. My son is the president of the hospital here. It pays to have connections at the top," he says with a wink.

"Oh, that's cool," I tell him. His son must be a really smart guy. I ask him how he knew I was in the hospital in the first place. Frank tells me he found out by accident. He was driving a different way to work because of a closed road, and the detour took him down my street. He saw the police cars and the ambulance. He saw my bike leaned up against the bush, and he recognized it from the graveyard. He said he got a bad feeling in his stomach, so he parked and started talking to the other people standing around watching. He got the whole story, even my name and where they were taking me.

"Wow," I say.

"Everything happens for a reason. I'm a big believer in destiny. I mean, what are the chances of detouring everyone to *your* street? And that *I'd* pass by and recognize your bike?"

This is all real nice and everything, but I'm starting to get weirded out. He's too nice. I'm not used to nice. I really don't know why he cares about me and my bike and my life. What's up with this guy? What's his deal?

"Sir, I'm not trying to be rude or anything, but why are you doing all this? The brown bags, the visit, that poem?"

Frank nods his head at me for a few seconds without saying anything. I must've stumped him.

"Well, you have asked a mighty big question there, young man. I have given that a great deal of thought lately. For a while, I didn't have an answer."

Whoa, he's already thought about it. Second time he's read my mind. Freaky shit.

"Why did I care about a young man I had never even met? Well, my wife died about five years back—love of my life, that woman. I live alone now. When you live alone, you have a lot of quiet time to get your thoughts straightened out, to clear your head. When Gloria was alive, I always used my time bumping around on that mower to think through a conversation or a squabble we'd had. Gave me time to work it all out in my head. I knew that's what you were doing there too. A man knows these things about another man. That's why I never intruded. I always liked seeing you there, doing your thinking and your reading."

This is unbelievable. *I* don't want to interrupt *him*.

"And the poem? Well, now, that's mighty personal. My uncle gave me that poem after I had my son. I tucked it away and never thought anything of it. I wasn't a poem kind of guy. And let's just say I wasn't the best father in the world. I was tough on Michael, real tough. Never laid a hand on him, but I used my words. Nothing that boy did was ever good enough for me.

"Got lots of regrets about my parenting." Frank presses his lips together, then turns and looks out the window. I'm not saying a word. He takes a big breath and says, "But regrets don't get you anywhere, no matter how much time you spend thinking them through on a mower. Best thing to do with a regret is to share it with the person, tell him how you feel, how you wished things could've been different. Won't do much for the other person, but it takes a breeze of guilt out of your hurricane. Just a breeze, though."

Incredible. Is this guy for real? I mean, he shows up out of the blue, and it's like he knows exactly what to say to me. Out of nervousness, I shift my weight in my wheelchair. A pain shoots down my bad leg. I cringe.

Frank is at my side before I can even exhale. "Are you all right?"

I nod, let out a long breath, and slowly get myself back into a comfortable position.

Frank waits. "You okay now?"

"Yeah, I'm good."

He sits back down. "I know you're still wondering why I gave you that poem. I apologize for my long-winded answer. I haven't spoken this out loud to anyone yet. You are the first person to hear my 'mower thoughts.'" He laughs.

I smile at him. He has the best voice. It reminds me of the grandfathers I used to see on television. Kind, patient, gentle.

Everything Pop isn't.

"Being the quiet type, I notice things. Now, I hope you don't think I'm prying in your private life or anything, but I noticed your bruises. I could see them across the cemetery. A young man doesn't get those kinds of bruises by accident. Not over and over again. And when your neighbors said it was just your mom and your grandfather living with you . . ." Frank's voice trailed off.

My smile disappears. I am not going to discuss my pop with this guy. I don't even know him. But I don't know how to make him stop talking.

"I've offended you. I'm sorry. I was just trying to help. This was a mistake. I'm sorry. I'll go." Frank stands up.

I don't want him to leave. I'm not sure why, but I don't.

"It's all right. I like the poem," I admit.

"I do too. I do too."

"My favorite part is the last line: 'Some wait for no one, they fill themselves up.' It makes me feel . . ." I don't know how it makes me feel. Feelings are new to me. I've always shoved them down and ignored them. I've never acknowledged them, let alone named them.

"Hope?" he asks.

I take a second and think about it, and yeah, that is the perfect word to describe how it makes me feel. I tell him this.

Victor walks in. His eyes are red and his face is blotchy. He's definitely been crying. I can tell he doesn't know what to do because he just stands there, staring.

Frank walks right up to him and introduces himself, and they shake hands. Victor sits on his bed with his back to us, but he doesn't pull the curtain closed. Normally, I'd bitch at Victor to close the curtain, but I can't take my eyes off of Frank. I study him. He moves slowly but with precision, and he smiles a lot. Not like a creepy clown or anything, a real-deal smile. And know it sounds crazy, but I swear to God his eyes twinkle.

Today has been a wild day. I just want to crawl into bed and relax. I get myself up on one leg. Frank says, "Would you like help getting into bed? I know I'm old, but I'm still pretty strong."

I almost say no, but then I tell him sure. He helps me up and tucks me under the blankets. For real.

Frank holds out his hand, and I grab it. We shake, and he says, "Rest up. And tonight, dream of hope." Then he squeezes my shoulder.

When he walks out, I wonder when I'll see him again, because I want to.

K. M. Walton

# Victor

I GUESS THAT WAS BULL'S GRANDFATHER. NOT WHAT I pictured in my head at all.

"He's not my grandfather," Bull says from his bed.

Weird.

"Oh," I say nonchalantly, trying to act as "whatever" as possible. This is the first thing Bull Mastrick has ever said to me that wasn't evil.

I'm sitting on my bed with my back to him, and I look at my watch. Ten minutes until my follow-up appointment with the psychiatrist. Everyone says the ticket out of here is to say the right stuff. Lacey gave me all the buzzwords yesterday. She said Kell told them to her in the one and only verbal interaction they've ever had. I'm definitely done with this place, even though that scares the hell out of me. I'm done.

Agnes is at the door and tells me I have a phone call.

"My mother?" I ask.

"Nope, Patty Cullen," she replies before turning to leave.

I am in shock for a few reasons:

1. This means everyone in school must know what I did, and

2. Patty Cullen is calling me. In the crazy house. Me, Victor Konig, is being called by a girl. And not just any girl. A really pretty girl from school. That girl is on the phone. Right now.

Agnes leans in our doorway again. "You having a hearing issue, Victor?"

I do not want to annoy Agnes. I jump up and follow her down the hall. I don't have any thoughts right now. My head is blank, like someone wiped me clean. I have no idea what I'm going to say to Patty Cullen. Then guilt pokes at me because I feel like I'm betraying Nikole. But that's stupid. Nikole went back to her life, where she's popular and her friends call her Queenie, and she'll have another hot guy after her in, like, two seconds. Nikole told me to be happy. She told me to live because I'm worth it.

Agnes huffs with a smile. Then she hands me the phone, pats me on the back, and tells me to just be myself. Great, Agnes has figured out I'm a loser without me even saying a word.

"Hello?"

"Victor?" Patty sounds as nervous as I am.

"Yeah, hi. Is this really Patty?" I ask. I have to ask, even though I know it's her. I don't want to be tricked or fooled. Not now. Not today.

"Uh-huh, it is. Are you okay? I've been thinking about you."

Now, she's said this to me once before, the day after I passed out on my lunch tray. She said she was thinking about me; I remember that. So that means she's thought about me, like, twice. That's a lot, right?

"Really? You've been thinking about me?" I guess I just need to be completely sure about everything.

I hear her laugh, then she clears her throat. Patty breathes into the phone and then says, "Yeah, I have. Are you okay, Victor? Because I want you to know something."

This could be good. Or bad. Probably bad. She's probably going to tell me the whole school laughed their asses off at my botched demise.

"You still there?" she asks after a moment.

"Sorry, yeah, still here."

"Well, how are you really doing, Victor?"

That same feeling washes over me—the same feeling I got when I was on the phone with my nana. I really am okay.

I tell her, "I'm okay."

"You are? Seriously? Because I was beyond worried. You are always in class, so when you weren't there for the last day of school, I had this horrible feeling that something was wrong. I went to the guidance counselor, and she promised me she'd look into it. When word got out about you, and about Bull, at the end-of-the-year parties, I freaked out, Victor."

"So everyone at school knows what I did?"

"Everyone was really upset about it. Honest."

I don't say anything. The reality of having to go back to school in September crashes into me like a linebacker. I know I still have two-and-a-half months of summer vacation, but I don't want to go back to school ever. No one has noticed me for years, and now I'll be stared at and whispered about. I don't want to see any of those people.

"Hey? Listen, okay? I'm here for you. I've sort of had a thing for you. My friends always talked me out of saying something. But it's my life, you know? And I am making you a promise right now on this phone. I am here for you, okay?"

Holy crap. Patricia Cullen just told me that she has a thing for me. I jam my elbow into my thigh to see if I'm dreaming. Nope, awake.

"Victor, you're very quiet. You there?"

"Yes, I'm here."

"Are you freaking out?" Her voice cracks at the end. She sounds worried.

This is too much for me. This will never work when I'm out there, with people. "No, I'm not—, " I start. Then I have an immediate change of heart. Must be the courage juice. "Look, Patty, I've been through a lot, and I've grown up a lot in here, which is weird because it's only been a few days. I met this girl, and . . ."

"Oh, oh, I'm . . . wow, I'm sorry. I guess I never expected . . . oh, wow," she stumbles.

I am ruining this. "No! No! Let me finish, okay?"

"Go ahead," she whispers.

"I met this girl in here and she told me to stay alive. She told me I'm worth it."

"And you're going out with her?"

Still ruining this.

"No. What I'm trying to say is, she made me stop feeling invisible to the world. It's almost like she filled in the white spaces with color or something. And she made me want to live."

"And you're going out with her?"

"No, I'm not going out with her. She's already gone. She left this morning. But she made me want to live. I want to live. And I want you to be there for me. I want *you* to be there."

"I *am* here for you."

Not ruined. So not ruined.

# Bull

SOME DOCTOR COMES IN AND WAKES ME UP FROM my nap. He asks if I know where Victor is; he says he's late for his appointment. I guess he's the psychiatrist. I tell him Victor's on the phone. Then he wants to know how I'm doing. I zone in on his eyebrows as soon as my eyes are awake enough to focus. They are unbelievable. I tell his eyebrows I'm good, and I ask him when I can get out of here.

"Well, I think I owe you an apology, William," he says.

I squint. "For what?" What could this guy possibly have to apologize to me for?

"I apologize that we haven't talked yet. Both times I had

you on my schedule I had to deal with another patient's emergency. So, since I'm here and it's rather difficult for you to move around, why don't we have our session?"

I'm pretty sure he's talking about Andrew and his freakouts, which were both my fault. And *he's* apologizing to *me*. Classic. "Yeah, I guess," I say.

He picks up the phone and asks the nurse to tell Victor we'll need some privacy until he's finished the session. I swear his eyebrows tickle the receiver.

He hangs up, pulls my curtain closed, and says, "So, William, where is your head today? At this very moment?"

"Good."

"Good how?" he asks. He sits down in the chair in the corner.

"Good because I'll be getting out of here soon." I smile after the words leave my mouth.

"Have you had any thoughts of harming yourself while here?"

I shake my head.

"I'd like to hear you say it, William," he says.

I exhale through my nose and almost roll my eyes, but I catch myself. "No, I haven't had any thoughts of killing myself. Not one."

"Why do you think that is?"

"I don't know," I say.

"Well, if you did know, what would you say?" he asks

without moving anything but his mouth.

He is a strange man, but damn, he's good. I smile and nod to show him that I'm thinking. I look over his shoulder and out the window. I watch the summer clouds floating by all free and not connected to anything, and my answer just comes to me. "Well, I guess because I feel connected to living now."

He raises his eyebrows and I feel a breeze, I swear. "Go on," he says.

"Before I got here, I just sort of rolled through life—and I rolled over people, too. I wasn't connected to anyone. Or anything."

"And you feel connected now? Why do you feel that way?"

This guy doesn't quit, does he? I take a deep breath and pause. He waits. I puff my cheeks up and blow out a huge breath. "Probably because I know that other people have shitty lives too, that I'm not the only one, I guess."

"You guess? Are you sure, or are you still evaluating your feelings?"

I shrug my shoulders. What does this dude think I am, a genius?

"How do you feel about going home?" he asks.

"I don't know. Fine, I guess."

"Fine? Nothing is worrying you? Like, say, how you'll make it up the steps to your apartment?"

I squeeze *my* eyebrows together. How does he know this?

"I had a conversation with your mother and your grand-father about how you will navigate your apartment. They were at a loss. Your mother suggested you recover at a friend's house, but she failed to offer any feasible options or contact information. She said you have no other family in the area. So the social worker's been working on placing you in a reha-bilitation facility. You can't go home until you are able to use crutches to get up your stairs."

I am stuck on the part where my mother told him I should recover at a friend's house. She is too much. What friend? She knows I don't go anywhere. She knows I never have anyone over to our hellhole.

Then I get a crazy idea. Really crazy.

"Do you know Frank?" I ask him.

"Frank? Frank who?"

"Frank. His kid is the head of this place."

"Are you referring to our president, Michael Blessing?"

"Yeah. Yeah, he said his name was Michael. That's him."

He tells me he's confused and that he's not following my thinking here.

"Well, me and Frank are really good friends. I could stay with Frank."

There it is, the crazy idea.

"You are suggesting that I call the father of the president of the hospital and ask him to let you stay with him while you recuperate?"

"Yep, that's exactly what I'm suggesting." If I could hug myself right now I would.

"I'll have to speak to your mother about this. I assume she knows Frank as well?"

Shit. My mother could ruin this whole thing. I have to talk to her before he does.

"Oh, yeah, she knows Frank real well. She'll say yes; I know she will."

He's talking about papers needing to be signed and some other crap. I don't know. My head is spinning. He walks out, and I am left with my crazy idea. My hand is on the nurse call button faster than the bullet that went through my leg. I ask for help to get up and permission to use the phone. I haven't called anyone today, I remind her.

I pass Victor in the hall, and I tell him Dr. Eyebrows is looking for him.

When I get to the nurses' station, Ellie hops up and pushes me into the corner and winks. I dial my home number. "Mom? It's Bull. No, I don't know where that money is. I don't know; I guess you can cash it. Oh, you already did? Listen, I need you to do me a favor. . . ."

Cracked                                                      **291**

# Victor

DR. EYEBROWS ASKS ME A BUNCH OF STUPID QUESTIONS.

No, I haven't thought of killing myself today.

No, I don't want to die.

Yes, I want to go home.

My stomach relaxes with every answer I give. Then he tells me I am allowed to go home in the morning. As he fumbles with papers on his clipboard, I replay the conversations with my nana and Patty.

I can do this.

I can do this.

I think.

# Bull

MY MOTHER WAS DRUNK, SO IT WOULD'VE BEEN EASY
to talk her into anything. She slurred her permission and then
cried about the flowers dying—or maybe it was the towers
sighing. Who the hell knows what she said?

After I hang up, Ellie says, "What's got you so smiley?"

I roll back from the desk and turn my wheelchair around.
Ellie has her hands on her hips with her head tilted to the
side. I'm going to miss seeing her. This must show on my
face, because she says, "Uh-oh, you go from a smile to a frown
when you see me? That's not good. What, do I have broccoli
in my teeth or something?"

"No, your smile is perfect," I whisper.

Ellie leans down and we're face-to-face. She grins and says, "Then what's up, William?"

How can I tell her that I will miss her voice? Her beautiful face? The sound of her laugh? She has been incredibly nice to me *and* she's seen my private parts.

Ellie says, "Welllllll?"

If I've learned anything in this place, it's that you should say how you feel when you have the chance. Wait, did I really just have a deep thought? Me? I believe I did. I drop my eyes, because even though I'm going to say what I want to say, there's no way in hell I'll have the balls to look her in the eye when I'm saying it.

Baby steps.

"I'm going to miss you," I say. I can't believe I didn't explode. But I didn't. I'm still sitting in my wheelchair with hot Nurse Ellie bent down in front of me.

She puts a hand on my shoulder and whispers to me, "I am definitely going to miss you as well, William Mastrick. You are a very special guy." Ellie stands straight up, and I think she's going to cry. I definitely cannot keep my shit together if she cries. I nod and she nods back. Then she says in a soft voice, "Where can I take you, sir?"

My first instinct is to say *Back to my room*, but I know

I'll just cry like a baby, so I say, "The common room would be great."

Only Grant's in there when I get dropped off. And believe it or not, even with my zit-face comment, we play, like, five rounds of Crazy Eights. Perfect distraction. He's actually not a bad guy.

About twenty minutes later Dr. Eyebrows comes in and asks me to join him. He pushes me into his office and tells me he also got a hold of my mother and she said she was going to stop by tomorrow and sign the papers.

"The papers?" I ask.

"Yes, the papers. She's granting permission for you to be placed in another location. One that's easier for you to navigate."

"So I'm going to that rehab place?" I say, all defeated. I guess it's better than going home to Pop and his fists.

But the doctor is shaking his head. He tells me that he's also spoken with Frank, who has agreed to let me stay with him until I'm able to walk by myself. And that there is no need for me to be placed into a rehabilitation facility.

I pretend to cough so I can hold back the waterworks. One rebel tear leaks out and I swipe it away while the doctor is busy with his paperwork.

"Mr. Blessing would like to speak to you, Bull. Let me get you back to the phone." He wheels me back to the nurses' station.

The doctor looks at his clipboard, dials Frank's number, and hands me the phone. He smiles and pats me gently on the back. "Good luck, William."

"Hello?" Frank answers.

"Frank, it's Bu—I mean, *William* Mastrick."

"William, so nice to hear your voice. What do you think of staying with me for a while?"

I squeeze my eyes shut and hope my voice doesn't crack. My back is to the hallway, so I let the tears run down my face. "I . . . I think it's a great idea."

He laughs and I picture his twinkling eyes. I laugh along with him. He tells me he's going to spruce up his son's old room for me. He says he's going to stop by my house to pick up some things, and meet my mom and grandfather. I practically jump through the phone and tell him no.

"My mom's going to bring some stuff tomorrow when she comes to sign the paperwork."

That's all I would need: my shitfaced mother answering the door while my grandfather is spread all over the table, drunk. He'd see how I live. No way. Frank would call the whole thing off.

If everything works out, I'll be out of here tomorrow morning.

I think I can do this. And then I think of Kell.

# Victor

IT'S MY LAST NIGHT IN THIS ROOM, IN THESE SWEATS, in this place. I will only miss two things: Nikole and Ellie. Ellie said the nicest thing to me after dinner. She told me that I should keep looking people in the eye when I talk to them because I have kind eyes. She said my eyes are gentle.

"I'm going to miss you, Victor. You're a good guy. Stay strong when you get out of here. Okay?" Ellie said.

I looked her right in the eye and nodded. I couldn't talk because I would've started crying. At least I looked her in the eye. I know she understood me, because she nodded back and smiled. I'll never forget her.

As I stare at the ceiling, I think that maybe I'll miss Lisa; she got us to talk a lot. And it felt good to tell off Bull. Like a good brain scrub or something.

I wonder how it will be with Bull when we get out. I know one thing: I am done letting him wreck me. I haven't thought about how I'm going to handle him if he starts with me out there. But I know I'm not going to take it, like I used to.

I won't.

I also wonder how it'll be to have my nana live with us. I know my parents will probably be mean to her. But after talking to her on the phone, I know she can take them. I am just glad I won't be alone with them in that house, in my life, anymore. She'll be there for me. A buffer. An ally. She said so.

Regardless, I won't let my parents run my life. I am going to stand up to them and their unreasonable expectations. I am going to advocate for myself. That's what the doctor told me to do. I'm willing to learn, which is a huge change in my thinking.

I see therapy in my future.

I turn over in bed and stare at the curtain. Patty's smiling face comes to mind for some reason. I replay the end of our conversation. She said she'd meet me in the park my first day back home. She said she had something for me. I can't wait to see her, but I'm worried. What if I clam up and have nothing to say? Four days in here did a lot for me, but I'm still *me*. Shy, unsure, confused. I hope once she sees me, she won't change her mind about me.

Deep down, I don't think she will.

# Bull

KELL.

How am I going to leave her? I can't leave her in here all alone. I don't even know where she lives. What kind of boyfriend am I?

After I hang up with Frank, I ask Agnes to wheel me back to the common room. She checks her watch and says, "It's almost time to go back to your rooms for the night."

"How long do I have?" I ask.

"Fifteen minutes or so."

"I just want to see if someone's in there." She makes her lips tight and then nods. In the short ride from the nurses' station I wonder how I'm going deliver this bomb of awful news to Kell. What am I going to say?

Agnes pushes me in and announces, "Fifteen minutes, you two."

Grant's gone and it's just Kell in there, alone in the corner, facing the window. Like always. She startles at Agnes's voice.

"Hey," I say.

She sees me and hops up. She takes my face in her hands, bends down, and kisses both cheeks. I wish I could pull her onto my lap and just make out with her.

"Hey," she says, "I missed you."

"I missed you, too."

How am I going to tell her that I'm leaving tomorrow? What if she freaks out and tries to hurt herself? I don't think I could handle that, knowing that she killed herself over me. Whoa. Wait a second. That's a pretty big thing to do, right? Kill yourself over some dude you just met? Who do I think I am? Like she would hurt herself over me.

"So, how did it go with Psycho-Brow?" she asks. "Grant told me he saw him wheeling you around earlier."

"I'm leaving tomorrow."

Wow, that was as smooth as sand. What a moron.

She gives me the straight-armed double finger. Again.

"WAIT! Don't walk away from me!" I yell at her.

She turns around, crosses her arms, and glares at me.

"Listen, when you get out of here, we'll meet up. And there's the Internet; we can Skype, and . . . well . . . I've heard it's like you're in the same room with the person. I'm not going to lose you, Kell."

This isn't working. She hasn't blinked once.

"You are a cool girl. And you are the smartest person I've ever met; your book is going to be something. You make me feel important. And this is really hard stuff for me to say out loud to you," I admit.

A few blinks. Good, maybe she's melting a bit.

"And you have the most amazing breath. Do you know it smells like vanilla? And when you kissed me . . ." I don't think I can say what I want to say.

"I use vanilla-flavored toothpaste. And when I kissed you . . . what?" she says.

"I think I fell in love with you."

*Epilogue*

# Victor

IT'S BEEN FOUR MONTHS SINCE I TOOK MY MOTHER'S pills. My parents came home from Europe the week after I got out of the ward. They unpacked obnoxious amounts of new things from their trip. I got a Leaning Tower of Pisa magnet. Some things never change.

Except, actually, a few things *have* changed. My nana is like the voice I never had. She barks at my parents every time they say something to me that she doesn't like. She told them they should be thrilled with how I did on my SAT and got them to stop the tutor.

And last month during dinner, my grandmother took her

fork and gently tapped on the side of her water goblet. "I have an announcement to make." She firmly explained that she had set up counseling for me and my parents. Together.

Oh, my parents vehemently opposed the idea at first. But my grandmother is one stubborn old woman. And now we go, all three of us, once a week.

Our counselor is this young hippie named Autumn, who smells like the incense from church and has extremely loving views and opinions on parenting. In other words, she's the polar opposite of my parents. During today's session, Autumn looked wide-eyed at my mother and said, "Wait a second, you mean to tell me you do not hug this incredible son of yours every single day?" And then she created this whole playacting thing where she made both of my parents hug me and not let go for an entire minute.

I swear I felt warmth coming from my mother for the first time.

Autumn is pretty much a genius, and she knows exactly how to chip away at my parents' plastic exteriors. We all have to keep journals and write to each other every week on the question or topic she gives us, and then we exchange the night before the session.

My dad has sort of opened up to me on those pages.

We got a new dog after I wrote about how much I

missed Jazzer. My father took me to pick him out. And since my mother made so much progress in the not-being-such a-complete-bitch department, I chose another small dog—not a teacup, I couldn't do it—a little Bichon Frise puppy, whom I named Harry. You should see how white and fluffy Harry is. My mother even loves him.

Patty Cullen did meet me in the park my first day back. We sat under a tree and talked for hours. She never looked more beautiful to me than she did that day. On the walk home she pressed a CD case into my hand and told me to listen to it before I went to bed. I remember asking her which song, and she told me there was only one.

I didn't wait until bed. After kissing and hugging my nana hello, I walked directly upstairs to my room and popped the case open. A folded paper lay on top. One side had the lyrics and the other had a handwritten note.

Dear Victor,

I am glad that you're still alive. I thought about you a lot. I even went to church to pray for you. I know you don't know me really well yet, but that was big for me, the

*going-to-church thing. When I
listen to Coldplay's "Everything's
Not Lost," I think of you. It
could—it should—be your theme song.*

*Love,
Patty*

She was right; it *could* be my theme song. I guess it actually is, because I listen to it every morning before I leave the house. My favorite line is "If you think that all is lost, I'll be counting up my demons, hoping everything's not lost." At random times that line'll pop into my head and I'll smile, because I thought everything *was* lost. I believed it. But it turns out it wasn't. Patty found me.

Patty's note, Patty's kindness, Patty's acceptance, Patty's eyes, Patty's lips, Patty's hands, Patty . . . I appreciate and love each of these things. Patty Cullen is my miracle.

The easiest thing right now is spending time with Patty. Sometimes, when we're on the phone, Patty whispers that she can't stop thinking about me. I always whisper back that *I* can't stop thinking about *her*. Last night I told her I loved her for the first time. She said she loved me too. It was perfect.

Nikole and I have kept in touch online. She started dating

one of Greg's best friends almost as soon as she got out of the ward. His name is Balls. For real. Well, it's his nickname, anyway. She swears in true Lacey style that he is "the one" and that they're sure Greg set them up from heaven. I will always love what she did for me—how she believed in me, acknowledged my existence, and treated me with dignity. Always.

And Bull Mastrick has stayed away from me since school started. It's like we understand each other. We don't talk or anything, but there's this acceptance between us. We both know the other's pain. Sometimes in the dark, just before I fall asleep, I'll think I hear Bull rustling his covers, and then I come to. I always lie there and think about how we were both in such awful situations, each losing bits of our self along the way. Ending up in the ward was the best thing that ever happened to me because I was able to gather up those bits of *me*.

I'm nearly whole right now. I'm all right.

*Epilogue*

# Bull

I'VE BEEN OFF THE CRUTCHES FOR ALMOST A MONTH. Had my cast off for two. It's crazy how you can hardly tell when you look at my leg. I feel pretty strong again.

Frank is a really good guy. He treats me like his own son. He said he actually treats me better than his own son. When I first got to his house, we stayed up late almost every single night talking about stuff. He was cool with everything. I told him the whole story. The real story.

Two days later, when we were eating breakfast, he said, "I wanted you to have that poem so you'd know—"

I waited a few seconds. "So I'd know what?"

He cleared his throat. "So you'd know it doesn't have to be like that. That when you grow up, you don't have to be like them—your grandfather and your mother. You can be better than them."

About *them* . . . my mom never dropped anything off when she signed the papers for me to stay with Frank. She told Dr. Eyebrows she couldn't find anything *to* drop off. I remember laughing and saying, "Typical." Frank told me not to worry, and he took me to get a whole mess of clothes. Like I said, he's a really good guy.

After I was all healed up, I was supposed to go home, but my pop died. He choked on his own puke at the kitchen table. My mom found him when she got home from Salvy.

The last time I talked to him was the day with the gun. I didn't get to say good-bye, but I'm not too broken up about it. He never even called me while I was in the nuthouse, not once during the whole five days. I know what he did for me, though. I know he told the police I tried to kill myself so I wouldn't go to juvie. I know that.

Frank took me to the funeral parlor to see Pop, and it was just me, my mother, and Frank. That's it. My mom had the smarts to *not* have a service, so the three of us just stood over his open coffin and said whatever we wanted to in our heads. I'm sure what I said in my head was way different from what my shitfaced mother mumble-jumbled in hers.

But Mom's in AA now. Frank told her, right there with my dead grandfather in front of us, that the only way he'd let me go back to her was if she went to AA. So now she goes every day. She says it's the only way she won't drink. To tell you the truth, she's not too bad when she's not wasted. To be honest, I couldn't believe she wanted me back. We still go at it sometimes—it's usually over folding the clean laundry or not having enough milk or some shit like that. But at least I have one parent that kind of gives a crap about me. I gave up that whole beach-reunion-with-my-father pipe dream.

Living in the apartment isn't that bad either. My mom cleared out Pop's room and gave it to me. I have my own room. Frank bought me my own bed and dresser because he said I deserved something to call my own. It's pretty cool to have my own stuff. Pop's bedroom always smelled like beer and urine, but now it smells like me.

I visit Frank every day after school, and we have dinner together. I do my homework over there sometimes too. My mom has been working the late shift; she says it helps her not drink.

I'm not as pissed off at the world anymore, but I still get mad when I think about the hell my pop put me through. At night sometimes I wake up sweating and junk because I expect him to come barreling in here and find me in his room. And beat the shit out of me.

That happens a lot.

But one good thing: I don't bother with anyone at school. Not even Victor. We sort of keep to ourselves. We both know a lot about each other, how messed up we were. Like, emotionally and stuff. And being in the ward made me realize that everyone has shit to deal with. I don't want to be the asshole anymore. I really don't.

Kell . . . well, Kell and me keep in touch online. We e-mail a lot. She's the one who told me about Andrew—how he found his stepdad's old hunting rifle in the back of the garage and blew his head off, right there with the lawn mower and boxed-up Christmas decorations. That story bummed me out for a long time.

Kell started a new book. It's based on her, and she sends me every chapter. I'd be bold-faced lying if I said I haven't cried while reading every chapter. She's sent me fourteen chapters so far, so that's fourteen crybaby sessions.

She wants to be a real writer—like, make money for what she writes. I tell her all the time that her brain churns out words more smoothly than freaking Willy Wonka churns out chocolate. She's that good at it. And one day I know I'll be able to buy one of her books in the bookstore.

Kell's in an outpatient treatment program; she goes twice a week. The court wouldn't put her back with her stepdad because he was doing horrible things to her, so she's with some foster family. She says they're nice enough and they all keep their hands to themselves, but she can't wait to turn eighteen so she can be on her own.

And yeah, I still love her. She loves me too.

I'm seeing her next Saturday. Frank's going to pick her up and bring her back to his house so we can hang out. How cool is he? He even helped me plan out some stuff to make her feel really special when she gets there, like flowers and a poem.

And I go by William now. Even in school.

K. M. Walton

# Acknowledgments

Deep, deep appreciation goes to my very first readers of *Cracked*—family, friends, and BETAs alike: Nikole Becker, Mary Anne Becker-Sheedy, Meghan Becker Passarelli, Christina MacRae, Margie Pearse, Annemarie Paterni, Patty Scoboria Clark, Weronika Janczuk, Susan Mills, and Christina Lee. Thank you for sharing your outrageously encouraging thoughts and helpful opinions.

Thank you to my faithful (yet small) horde of blog readers and Twitter followers. Just so you know, my heart leaps every time I see a new comment or response from any of you fine people. Keep 'em coming. It makes me happy.

To my fellow 2012 debut authors over at The Apocalypsies, thank you for all of your support, sharing of knowledge, excitement, and friendship. Visit http://apocalypsies.blogspot.com to meet everyone—they're quite a group!

Thank you to the wonderful Goehler family for allowing me to put Greg's real and tragic story into this book. I will never forget.

To fellow writer and friend, Christina Lee, thank you for suggesting we jump in a cab, 10:30 at night, in NYC, with no coats, at the January SCBWI Winter Conference, so I could stand in front of the Simon & Schuster building for a photo. One of my most treasured moments.

Thank you to my dear friend, Margie Pearse. Your continued belief that this would actually happen one day helped to fuel my persistence.

To my very large and very awesome family (the "other" Waltons and foreigners included), thank you for cheering me on with kind words, cards, e-mails, and phone calls. In short, my entire family rules. COUSINS! COUSINS!

Thank you to Gail and Frank Scarpa, my in-laws, for allowing me to hole up in your pool house during that long-ago Easter vacation, cranking out my first novel (not *Cracked*—it's a sci-fi). And thank you for believing this would happen one day.

To Meghan, Nikole, and Christina, my three younger sisters, you three are the most amazing, beautiful, supportive, hysterical, awesome, and steadfast best friends I will ever have. I love you, McGeedles, Niki-hoy, and Quitty.

Special thanks to my sister Nikole, *the* Nikole from the book. She really *did* lose her spectacular boyfriend, Greg, through that hideous tragedy. She's one heck of a woman and sister. For all the right reasons.

Thank you, Robert Charles Becker, my father, who passed away in 1997 at the age of fifty-one. I know you have silently spurred me on—pulling *heavenly* strings. I miss you, Dad.

Thank you to my incredible mother, Mary Anne Becker-Sheedy, whose beauty radiates both inside and out. Without you building me up since birth and *showing* me how to be a good human being, I would've never had the inner drive to write, especially this book. You've believed in me for . . . forever, and I love you. So much.

Thank you to my two spectacular sons, Christian and Jack. You know how much I love you both—I tell you every day. I'm certain there will never be two human beings that make me prouder to be alive. I thank God every night that *I* was chosen to be your mother. You are each a gift in your own way and have made this journey towards publication explode with genuine hope and excitement. Thank you both, my angels.

Thank you to the love of my life, Todd Walton. Who knew back in WCU's Sanderson Hall, room 714, circa 1987, that I had met my soul mate? Apparently my soul knew. Your smile (and steadfast belief in me) has the power to melt my silent fears and doubts, washing them down the drain where they belong. I am the luckiest woman alive to share this lifetime with you. I will love you so, for always.

Thank you to my lovely and brilliant agent, Sarah LaPolla. Your initial e-mail, after pulling me from your slush pile, has been dipped in gold and sprinkled with diamonds. Your insight, ideas, and guidance are equally as dazzling. Infinity-thank-yous for believing in my writing and ultimately believing in me. Synergy.

Thank you to my editor, the dedicated genius, Annette Pollert, for all of your hard work. You pushed my writing in directions I didn't even know existed. Thank you for loving Bull and Victor as much as I do. Wahoodles.

Thank you to the entire Simon Pulse team: Bethany Buck, Mara Anastas, Jennifer Klonsky, Dayna Evans, Russell Gordon, Lucille Rettino, Carolyn Swerdloff, Dawn Ryan, Paul Crichton, Mary Marotta, Christina Pecorale, Jim Conlin, Victor Iannone, Theresa Brumm, Mary Faria, and Alison Velea for all of your hard work and dedication. I am humbled.

Thank you to Coldplay, Radiohead, and Civil Twilight for creating their brilliant music that pumped through my headphones as I wrote this book. You rule on every level.

And finally thank YOU, reader, holder of my book. I sincerely hope you like(d) it, and I appreciate you choosing *this* book from the many.

PS, my sister Christina MacRae is the brilliant graphic designer of kmwalton.com. The woman is a freaking genius.